# Price

# of

# Refuge

Hypocrisy & Reality

Book:5

fiction

by

*'Videh'* Arvind Kumar

1968 to 1969

(a novel)

(class 6th)

(*Inaayatpur*)

## Dedication

*Price of Refuge*
*(Hypocrisy & Reality:*
*Book 5)*

*Dedicated to those wretched ones – children particularly – whose parents are incapable of providing them with basic necessaries of living, viz: food, clothing and shelter; and who by virtue of being dependent on others – including the so-called near relatives – for these basic requisites, fall prey to incest and sexual abuse at the latter's hands, unbeknown to the duffer unworthy parents!*

# Table of Contents

# *Copyright*

Price of Refuge
(Hypocrisy &  Reality:
Book 5)
First published in July, 2024
All rights reserved
@ *'Videh' Arvind Kumar*
Lucknow, India

## Preface

**'Price of Refuge'**, the fifth volume in the fiction series 'Hypocrisy & Reality' furthers the journey of the protagonist into the world where even after having spent a full year in exile with his maternal relatives when he returns to his paternal relatives, he finds to his dismay that his father is absolutely incapable of arranging a dwelling of his own, nor does the latter show any prospects of ever acquiring one, with the result that his unworthy father's retinue – the large family – is destined to stay in the vacant house of his elder brother, the house of the elder sister of the protagonist's mother.

And not to mention of the inexorable dent to the self-esteem and self-confidence of impressionable psyche of the children of such parents, he finds himself to be a mute subject to child abuse at the hands of none other than supposedly an elder cousin of his, the son of his so-called benefactors who provided refuge in their vacant house. And just beside his parents sitting on both the sides of the cot where he was being fucked by his elder cousin of far advanced age, of his father's age. Under the quilt in the winter season!

That was the price paid by the child for the indolence and handicaps of an unworthy father for seeking shelter under the tutelage of so-called relatives and not exerting for making his own arrangements. How can a person perform only one sided act of having sex and begetting issues without any concern for food, clothing and shelter for the hapless creatures that are produced as a result of the sexual activity of two fertile persons of opposite sexes in the wake of social ritual called marriage? Not only this, his sisters were abused too one by one by the same elder cousin nonchalantly – a paedophile as he was. It is not for nothing that the protagonist calls the person claiming himself to be his father as unworthy father and his mother as unworthy mother; or in sum, both of them as unworthy parents.

He has lost all faith in societal relationships and has developed a psychological complex, a phobia for close relations, whereby he dreads company of his elder relatives everywhere and throughout his later life, apart from developing a perennial tendency for self-sex and masturbation whenever he happens to recollect that shameless act of his devil cousin, his so-called refuge-giver. No refuge seemingly looking innocuous goes without some price to be paid either by self, spouse or one's children. Only fools and deranged persona like the protagonist's father think that everything is okay in seeking refuge, shelter or debt from society!

**गृहस्थ के धर्म:- महाभारत उद्योग पर्व**

पृथिव्याम् सागरान्तायाम् द्वाविमौ पुरुषाधमौ।
गृहस्थश्च निरारम्भ: सारम्भश्चैव भिक्षुक: ॥

*(समुद्र पर्यन्त इस सारी पृथ्वी में ये दो प्रकार के अधम पुरुष है:- अकर्मण्य गृहस्थ, और कर्मों में लगा हुआ सन्यासी।)*

द्रावेव न विराजेते विपरीतेन कर्मणा।
गृहस्थश्च निरारम्भ: कार्यवांश्चैव भिक्षुक: ॥
*(दो ही अपने विपरीत कर्म के कारण शोभा नहीं पाते:- अकर्मण्य गृहस्थ, और प्रपञ्चों में लगा हुआ सन्यासी।)*

*'Videh' Arvind Kumar*
*Aashrum, Lucknow, UP, India*
July, 2024

## Transcripts of *Hindee* letters and *maatraas*

Keeping in view the special pronunciations of *Sanskrit* words, and with a view to differentiating between the disparate pronunciations, we have followed the following regimen of transcription from *Devnaagaree* to Roman script. This clarification will help the readers appreciate the nuances of linguistic specificities and enjoy the text in truly desired sense. Moreover, the vernacular words, particularly nouns, have been italicized.

अ a, आ aa, इ i, ई ee, उ u, ऊ oo, ऋ ri, ए e, ऐ ai, ओ o, औ ऑ au, अं an, अ: :,

क ka, का kaa, कि ki, की kee, कु ku, कू koo, कृ kri, के ke, कै kai, को ko, कौ kau, कं kan, क: kah;

## 1. No Clue As To The Future
*Enter Protagonist*

First I might have stood in the class and topped I might have the Exam Centre in Standard Fifth, but the future for me was bleak nevertheless! There was no light at the end of the tunnel, nor in any direction whatsoever; and I had no inkling of it all at all. I was happy in my reverie, thinking that my *Naanaa-Naanee's* house was my own house, and that I was to stay there only for ever. Despite the fact that I had a dim idea that there was a gloomy prospect of returning to that hell hole of my paternal dwellings. The situation got aggravated with my father having made no progress in the past one year as regards construction of his nest. Nor was there any prospect whatsoever in the immediate or distant future!

What was being cooked I did not know but I was glad that I would go to *Jaabil* school from the coming year along with my two cousins – daughters of my two *Maamaajees* – who were of my age almost, somewhat elder, and were very affectionate as the siblings ought to be by nature. The *Jaabil* school was also very well managed one and very well kept; at least that was my impression.

When no development took place even during the summer vacations of the schools when my father would have visited his village, and should have thought something about his exiled family and their return, he seemed to be unconcerned, as if it were none of his business. He was correct at least in one respect, and that was that there was no dwelling space at his village for us, his family, hence where could he put us up even if he had chosen to summon us.

But the situation at my maternal household was getting precarious by the day. Not because they could not afford to feed us or clothe us moderately as well as they themselves did, but because the society was hell bent upon raising fingers on this extraordinary development whereby a married young girl had not been to her husband for past one whole year. And this was tantamount to divorce in absolute terms, albeit undeclared one. Who could clarify to them that there was no shelter left for these wretched lots in their paternal village? This was also not made clear or declared to villagers for fear of losing prestige in society and the village; for we were supposed to be as wealthy as our maternal households here were. And in my view that is sensible an approach, too, to marry one's issues in only wealthy families or in the families which have at least an equivalent level of living standards.

When the month of July approached and schools did open,

my maternal folks were in a quandary whether to admit me to *Jaabil* school or wait for my father to send a message concerning the latter's family. Ultimately, after much dilly-dallying, it was decided that I should be sent to *Jaabil* school, for it was not expedient to deprive a child, that too, a prodigy, a Centre-topper, of the schooling merely because his father was a non-fatherly stuff. No one could choose one's parents; whatever the Providence ordains one has to accept.

I was so glad to go to *Jaabil* school, especially, for my cousins and also many other good-mannered kids used to go to that school daily. *Jaabil* school's was a very impressive get up, and also, a set-up; its teachers were supposed to be very progressive-minded, and also, were gifted with dynamic personalities and progressive attitudes. Its Principal, or Head Master, as people called him, was a handsome youth whom the entire womenfolk adored as though! He was on the tongue of every woman folk even in our homestead at *Naanaa*'s, including my mother. I sometimes wondered why so much hype about a Head Master and what for? Actually, then I realised that he was of the same caste as we were, and was distantly related to the broader family tree. Nepotism was working at the back of everybody's

mind! Also, so blatantly getting displayed! Nevertheless, that was not the only reason: the school was kept well maintained, well decorated with flower-beds all around. I derived satisfaction from the fact that I would not have to go to the hell of my father's company, my equally cruel and harsh elder *Maamaa* being present here notwithstanding! But that was tolerable, for all other discomforts were taken care of, even as the other cares were none here! Moreover, here I saw that my mother could live happily and mirthfully. That was crucial for me. At my father's side she lived a life always with her face veiled, and also, ever under the scare of his insolent as well as tyrant husband. That was a big issue worth consideration.

The situation had reached such an imbroglio that it was essential to make arrangement for our shifting to our father's court, the village. My *Maamaajee* took initiative after much thought and pleaded with his younger sister and her husband, that is, my eldest uncle, who was incidentally *Badee Ammaa's* only son, to allow us to occupy their abandoned house at our village. After *Badee Ammaa's* demise last year that dwelling unit – a two room rustic, un-plastered set - was lying vacant, abandoned, unattended, and having turned into an abode for apparitions, spectres and fiends, as the conventional wisdom and local beliefs suggested.

I don't know whether motivated by my maternal uncle's goodwill based advice, or by the subconscious consideration that the dwelling unit would thus be taken care of and kept neat and clean, worthy of living, lest it should be turned into an uninhabitable place, they agreed to let us occupy their abandoned abode – *Badee Ammaa's* home. One more consideration working on their psyche might have been that in the eventuality of their denial to this exclusive proposition, their sister-in-law as well as the sister – the former in relation to the gent and the latter in relation to the lady -- would be obliged to stay away from her husband, burdened on her parents for another long year, that too, without any further clue to the future solution, if any, other than this one. And it would be indirectly due to their own actions whereby in the old *baakhar* they had cut the roof of the living hall in the middle resulting in the roof giving way and coming crashing down during the downpour. They were definitely accountable for the misery we were in. And the Providence helped us avenge them in this manner, in that they had to provide us their house, even though a deserted one, willy-nilly; the same house the construction of which had resulted in the cause of our present miseries

and the cause of collapse of our modicum common shelter!

Agreed, the sex is the causative factor of life - it's the sex and its concomitant procreative act only that produces the 'life', the conscious beings; nonetheless, to propagate the same 'life' what is quintessential is 'Food, Clothing and Shelter' only. Therefore, those who without having even the basic skills and wherewithal to afford the 'Food, Clothing and Shelter' do venture to produce issues unmindfully, are the biggest offenders, rather, sinners towards the living beings, i.e. those that get begotten in this process.

The normal tendency of Indians – the Indian society – is to get married, beget issues therefrom, then again arrange marriage for those begotten ones and ask the latter to beget more issues and so on…. Vicious cycle! To improve their economic or financial conditions has never been the priority of Indian society! They sort of love living in penury and wretchedness as though! Simply sub-human existence!

To paraphrase *Buddha*, in the human world, there are Four Societal Truths, viz;

**Misery:** It's only the 'food, clothing and shelter' which is the chief causative factor of misery for entire humanity! (The other species other than human beings do not suffer such a misery.)

**Misery has a cause:** Even without having the basic skills and any sort of wherewithal to afford 'food, clothing and shelter,' to get married and to beget innumerable issues and, that too, absolutely unmindfully!

**Misery has a remedy!**

**Remedy to misery is:** Simplest single-fold path: not to get married! (Instead, to channelise their energies towards arranging 'food, clothing and shelter' first!)

When we had no inkling that anybody, least of all our father, would ever come to take us to our village, one day it so happened that *Modhoo Chaachaa* was seen in our maternal uncle's village, unbidden and unexpectedly, of course, to my elder maternal uncle's great pleasure and satisfaction. And when he conveyed the message that he had come to take us to our father's village, my *Maamaajee* vented his pent-up ire against my father, and also, declared that he least minded keeping us – his sister's family – at theirs. He also proclaimed that he had planned, in case *Modhoo Chaachaa* did not come by, to allot some land in my name and arrange my marriage when the time came, thus settling us perfectly as well as permanently in their own village. In other words, he meant to convey to my father that even if his indolence was to be suffered they were willing to.

I was not happy to hear of this development, however, thinking that this elysian living in my maternal uncle's home would be snatched away from me, and we shall have to live with an indolent as well as rancorous soul in our village. Nevertheless, my mother was very happy, although her countenance pretended to be betraying nothing. She tried to look indifferent to the entire sensitive episode involving herself.

In the entire episode, I wondered why my father had not come personally to take us to his village; instead, why he had sent his cousin, his close relative to take us. I had never seen my father visiting his in-laws whereas all other in-laws and relatives of this family used to visit the village gladly. There was something glaringly missing in the personality and demeanour of our begetter, rather, father by accident, so to say.

XXX

*Enter protagonist*

With our departure from the maternal establishment along with *Modhoo chaachaajee* our maternal relatives would have heaved a sigh of extreme relief; relief not at getting rid of three or four souls -- of which, at least two were merely toddlers, girls – but because the scar of my mother's husband having forsaken my mother had ultimately seen a possibility of getting wiped off. When we left *Nanihaal,* I was not particularly enthusiastic, for the atmosphere to me at my paternal village seemed to be quite horrifying, scary, and also, suffocating; scary and horrifying because of the presence there of the entity which was called my father, and suffocating because there were so many restrictions on movements and conducts of ladies of the house. When ladies were ever under long veils, the children of their mothers were bound to feel suffocated; no soul would like to see one's mother under veil and living under so many draconian injunctions. On top of that, the entity called my father was the extreme point of that hypocrisy; he might be likened to the *Taalibaan* of present day world. I don't know whether *Taalibaan* have learnt from my father, or he was the precursor to *Taalibaan* in *Afghaanistaan.* Nonetheless, I can see the similarities so vividly between the two phenomena at this stage and my age.

From the maternal village, we were driven by *Rehloo* on the dusty path via the village of *Naglaa,* and if I am not amiss, under what impression I don't know, my elder maternal uncle kept on criticising my traits to *Modhoo chaachaajee*

throughout the way to railway station at *Daanwar.* I was so brilliant and it had been testified by my school teacher and fellow students, yet the wretchedness of living in refuge even as of blood relations engenders bad blood amongst the refugees and benefactors. After all, they were not keeping us of their own sweet will, or willingly, rather, we had been thrust upon them by our father unabashedly, or unashamedly.

We reached our village; it was merely two stations in between, although at that age the distance seemed like we were going to some foreign land, and the pangs of such separations and see-offs amongst both those going and those staying back were used to be heart-wrenching. Getting down at the non-descript railway station – *Cholaa,* named after the Southern dynasty of the yore -- from where we got the *ekkaa* - the horse-driven cart – to our town, we undertook small journey which again seemed very long as well as unpleasant. Ahead, at the town, there was no wherewithal to get a bullock-cart for ferrying us to our village, and *Modhoo chaachaajee* suggested that we hired an *ekkaa,* again, which he arranged on hire with the nod of my young mother. *Modhoo chaachaa* himself was a lad only at that time.

Even though we lived in village, even as our wider family

circle was all agrarian, even as we did not have any link whatsoever with the urban environs, still we, particularly the small set up of my father's family, were a perfect misfit in the village environs; nothing of our living conditions and styles resembled the living style of villagers. For instance, the commuters from town to village were supposed to be driven by bullock-carts, for villagers mostly owned their bullock-carts and their wards had the self-esteem of riding them. But we never had that luxury of being driven in a bullock-cart from town to village. Seemingly trifling, the phenomenon itself added a lot of respect to the person's status, for it reflected on the resourcefulness and financial status of the family. That way we always felt an inferiority complex as children. However expensive a *tongaa* or *ekkaa* you may hire and pay the fare, but it immediately betrays your lack of resources and lack of enterprise. A hired service can't match the prestige that is associated with an owned possession, and can never give one that type of sense of self-esteem. However beauteous a prostitute might be and whatever high price one might pay or squander on her dedication to one, one can never feel the pride that one feels when in company of one's own wife!

The hiring charges of the *ekkaa* were made to be paid by my mother, and that was symbolic of the inconsequentiality of all the relationships as regards monetary matters. And immediately on reaching the village, this signified a dent to the paltry sum in the wallet of my mother, and the beginning of the end of that money.

Father was not present there when we reached home, the home where once *Badee Ammaa* resided almost a year or so back, and I set off recollecting how I used to visit her off and on. Now we were going to live in the same house, in her house for good, who knows. We could never have envisaged that the turn of events would make us live there, or ever the house of *Badee Ammaa* would one day – so soon after its construction a while ago – be our dwelling place. However, life is mysterious like that only! Anything is possible in life! On this planet!

The house was in shambles, in a state of utter disrepair. Entirely dirty, dust-covered all around. Abandoned! Sort of haunted – *Bhutahaa*!

Our saviour who had brought us till this spot had already left for his own home. His brief was upto this point only. He was now no more bothered, we felt; on the way, we were feeling as though he would help us in all our travails at village, too. Soon we were disillusioned.

Of course, when he had reached our *Nanihaal*, I had wondered why he only always came to take my mother to her in-laws; why my father, her husband, never came to take her with him himself. That itself was a big abnormality betraying something abnormal about my father's personality and mental build.

At this home, we were left to fend for ourselves virtually, as we all felt including my mother. There was no drinking water. There was no arrangement for cooking food. Why only drinking water, there was no water at all, even for using in the loo, even as, there was no loo or toilet as such, and we had to go to the open fields for excreting. That was the norm, of course, nothing unusual about it; but there as well water was needed for cleansing the soiled buttocks after throwing away the night soil.

For a moment my mother screened everything with a sense of awe, pique and bewilderment. Her facial condition and the lines emerged on her beautiful forehead told the entire tale of woe she was finding herself suddenly in. She was coming from a house where there was no hint of any shortages or wretchedness. Here, she was an entirely destitute housewife, wife of a man who was the indolence

incarnate, and a demon incarnate as far as demeanour went. Totally insensitive and senseless!

The house was found locked, and it was only *Modhoo chaachaa* who had fetched the keys from somewhere. The keys might have been procured from the owners during the summer holidays gone by, and under the understanding reached might have been kept with our father.

Not finding our father at the site, we the kids and, especially, I felt relieved, for the presence of father at the scene was like the inferno ablaze. He was in the habit of flaring up without any cause alike a petrol can on seeing the matches. Rather, he could flare up even without a matches, figuratively!

Now, the first task at hand as we thought was to arrange for water; that was the be all and end all of all the other tasks. Although a dug well was there at a stone's throw almost in front of the house, we thought it expedient to activate the hand-pump that was available in the house itself. We children – I at eleven and my younger sister of six – were very glad to get our own house – a pucca one – and a hand pump and all that. Those were all unimaginable luxuries for us. Now, we would have our own hand-pump to fetch water, we were pleased to contemplate. So both the siblings started tinkering with the hand-pump. It was nonetheless beyond repair. Having remained in the state of perfect disuse for last one year or so, all its mechanical parts had dried and gone beyond repair. We brought water from the well and tried to make it functional, but in vain. Initially, when the water came out of the pipe of the hand-pump, there came out the tiny fishes from the spout of the pump to our bewilderment and dread. The water had become non-veg! We thought.

But the fishes all gone, there was no water yet. After some time, *Modhoo chaachaa* came, also came along his younger sister – *Deshraanee buaajee*; actually, their mother had been in some near relationship with my mother. That's why so much care! When they finally came to give their hand of support, that proved to be a lot of support for us, the beleaguered lot. Ultimately, with his experienced hands, the uncle – *Modhoo chaachaa* -- was able to activate the hand-pump and with that first accomplishment we became so happy. He in fact had to open the head of the pump and change its washers *et al.*

As soon as the water started coming out of the snout of the small hand-pump, both of us siblings became so happy as if we had attained *Nirvaan!* That was a perfectly novel experience for us wretched kids: water coming out of

our own pump! And our own house, so to say, even as at the back of our mind we had the nagging impression that it was not our own house, nor the water pump was ours. Nonetheless, we were being given the impression that the owners of the house – our aunt and our uncle, i.e. our mother's sister and her husband, or so to say, my father's elder brother and sister-in-law – who lived for service at *Ajmer* would never happen to come back from there and the house would eventually turn out to be our own. But was that true? No! All the surmises of human beings prove to be far-fetched only, eventually!

Thus, we started living in that house treating it as our own house. There is a saying that fools live making their own heaven out of hell, or out of nowhere; likewise, we the childish souls started living making our own heavens in a refugee house.

Water was fetched from the dug well, for the water that came out of the hand-pump was saline and not palatable to drink. We thought nonetheless that with the continuous usage of the hand-pump the taste of water would improve and would become sweet, but it never did. We rather became used to drinking the same saline water for years together thereafter. Strangers coming from outside found the water very undrinkable in taste in fact. We however had no other option. We kept on drinking that salty as well as saline water all along.

Food was cooked and we ate it. Village women who came to know of our mother's arrival started coming to see her. My mother, I have the vivid impression, had a very good image amongst the ladies of the village: image of a suave, sober and gentle lady, and a pretty one at that. However, just the opposite of the image of her husband, who was reviled by one and all, both men and women in the village. Although he was highly respectable outside his home.

Mother had come up with some provisions from her parents that could do for a day or two, and thereafter it was upto our father to arrange all the things.

In the meantime, however, our father had also emerged on the scene. He was, of course, pleased to see his grown up son and a lovely daughter after such a long gap. And, of course, his wife, that was long forsaken and separated. I observed that when my father met my mother they were both blushing as if in the feeling of intense love. That was another-worldly experience for me. I could never imagine my father showing affection and love towards my mother. I had always seen him behaving like a devilish creature, always behaving irrationally as well as insensitively. Now, by look itself

he did not look as if he were going to be of any help to us monetarily or otherwise; rather, he was depending for all the immediate needs to be fulfilled as regards household chores on the paltry sum in the tattered wallet of my mother as usual. He had no money at all at that crucial juncture when we arrived at our refugee camp.

XXX



### 3. Fruit Orchard As Firewood

*Enter protagonist*

First day's food somehow could be cooked with the courtesy of the relatives; they provided fire-wood, they provided spices, potatoes – potato is the only vegetable in the villages – and other paraphernalia of immediate requirement. My mother had her utensils and cooking implements kept in safe custody with someone and those were taken back, and washed. The brick and mud hearth *(choolhaa)* was somehow made functional. It was not such a simple enterprise as simple as this sentence is! We had to exert a lot, we had to improvise a lot, and also, we had to entreat a lot to our neighbours!

We had a fire-place (the *choolhaa*) on which food was cooked with the help of fire-wood. And on the first day itself the realisation dawned upon us that we had no fire-wood. One might wonder why we didn't have firewood; we were farmers after all, agriculturists, and a farmer's family is supposed to face no dearth of fuel or fire-wood. Well, we were farmers for name's sake only in fact. Nor did our father like to be treated like or called a 'farmer'. Given the choice he would have hidden himself from the scene of farms; he was so averse to anything to do with crops, fields or agriculture. Therefore, no question of there being a twig of trees in our homestead. My father believed in 'purchasing' everything. In 'purchasing' whatever was required! No need to grow it oneself, or do it oneself, using one's own two hands!

So when the issue of *Jalaawan* (fire-wood) arose, he first tried to trivialise it, as if it was so trivial an issue, rather no issue, so to say, but notwithstanding it seeming to be so trivial and a no-brainer, it had grave as well as immediate ramifications. How to cook food on the hearth without *Jalaawan?* For my father in his student life – a failed one, of course – had depended on kerosene stove or the dust-wood stove, he tried to make do with those contrivances first of all. That betrayed his lack of sense of proportion in fact. Making do with a stove for a single person may be alright; however, applying the same tenet to the entire large family establishment signifies craziness as well as lack of sense of proportion on the part of the possessor of such

notions. The laws of Nature, or physics, for that matter, that apply to large bodies do fail when it comes to subatomic particles; they assume an entirely spooky aspect in that the classical world metamorphoses itself into the quantum world.

The neighbours however were kind, and also, they were wary of the idiosyncrasies and craziness of this man, my father, they provided us immediate succour by extending support, yet they suggested to our father that he'd better arrange for a large quantity of fuel wood from somewhere immediately. For he had no prospects of getting wood in future also from anywhere for he did not do farming. Fuel supply was interrelated with farming; everything in rural milieu is so closely interrelated.

And quick came the relief as though from the side of Providence. An orchard – a garden of fruit trees – was being felled in front of our dwelling unit at a small distance, almost half a kilometre away. The owners were constrained to destroy the orchard for retrieving the cultivable land under the pressure of growing number of issues in the ever widening family fold. Fields were required to grow cereals which had come to be regarded as the only sustainable staple food for families. With the nascent Green Revolution this was a novel development. Fruits had lost primacy in the food platter of rural families. Little did they know that food is not merely the consuming of cereals and potatoes, rather, it comprises a sensible set of nutrients, too. But who cares for sensibility or health? That's taken as a given!

The logs of the fruit trees and other trees were taken away by the wily carpenters and it was decided that they would give the plentiful of twigs to our father. Let me hasten up: 'giving' in rural environs meant 'to sell for money'. Nothing comes for free in the rural arena, however queer or paradoxical it might sound. When the bullock-cart full of twigs arrived at our house, we were very glad, for in our childishness we thought, the fuel was more than enough forever. It, however, was not so; it soon proved wrong. Also, we thought that it was given free of charge, out of magnanimity of the well-acquainted villager, but when our father disclosed that one or two hundred rupees were to be forked out in due course, our hearts got sunk. Even those who spoke amiably and seemingly favourably as if those were our best well-wishers did so with a view to making some money out of our flesh! Anyway, there was no way out of this morass, too. Father was too happy to 'buy' all that residue of the felled fruit garden. He seemed to be little bothered about the quantity of money to be paid for that; he seemed to be more pleased to get an opportunity to 'buy' one more item, and in the process run one more 'debt'. For he held that it betrayed his 'creditworthiness' amongst the local folks, and he didn't even flinch from boasting of this trait of his personality. How foolish!

Now in hindsight I can recall that father had never been able to repay that amount, rather, he had ultimately borrowed from someone else at a high rate of interest of 60% per annum, i.e. 5% per month, to repay this amount, and that habit eventually turned out to be endemic for him for whole of his life and the family.

The seemingly bountiful of firewood was piled up in front of the house and fenced by a rope so as to check the pilferage by petty thieves. This *Lakshman-Rekhaa* of rope could be effective only against saints but not against *Raavans*. How could a weak rope tied around a huge pile of twigs and slender branches of mango trees check the thieves or petty pilferers from stealing small quantities on daily basis in the evening or in the dead of night? The happiness of getting rid of anxiety for fuel remained but for a few months and the pile of fuel was soon depleted, for the users were many even as stealthy ones.

XXX

*Table of Contents*

### 1. Eyes Opened To Natural Cleansing

*Enter protagonist*

The new house, or refugee shelter, to be precise, we entered in was a totally new environment for us kids: it was hot, humid and sultry all around. Yet there was no dearth of zeal in our hearts. There were two huge *Neem* trees in front of the house; very huge indeed from the perspective of us children. They were the only relief for us from the scorching sunrays and the dreary surroundings. They provided us the much needed shade for most part of the weary day. Also, they looked like two sentinels, two living entities protecting and standing guard to our tiny family, giving the impression as if two of our ancestors were watching and assuring us from above. For, to testify to our childish assumptions there were many types of birds roosting there, or did temporarily visit and perch on their twigs off and on. Their activities and queer sounds for us were nothing short of melodious music, and a whole mysterious world apart from our own childish world. Their lives were complementary to the lives of us human souls, equally significant and equally vibrant. Sometimes methinks that had there not been the presence of those supra-human entities around, how dreary would our existence have been in that eventuality in those environs!

The seasons change, the weathers do change; even the occurrences change from day to day. In our case, even the topography and the geography had undergone a drastic change. Even so, our financial status had dwindled alarmingly. Under the guardianship of our maternal relatives we were totally immune from such vagaries as we had to face here at every step and every day, virtually without exception. The change of circumstances and all that ultimately told upon our health in the form of diseases erupting through various organs of our toddler's or teenager's bodies. The water that was saline also would have taken its toll on both our anatomy and our psyche. We were permanently melancholy as regards prospects for sweet water ever in future. We had resigned to the idea of never having the sweetness of water; which figuratively was as though an indication of the flavour of our lives that were to be lived there, in that refugee home. A saline existence! A salty existence! We never tasted any sweetness while living there in our lives, too.

The family establishment had taken a shape, and also, a semblance of social linkages had been established. That felt like us having been jointed with a twig of the big tree and having started blooming. After a week or so, for we – my sister and I - were too much exposed in our overenthusiasm to sunshine, also possibly due to finding us in our supposedly own house – an entirely novel feeling for us poor kids - there started the eye disease – eye sore, the conjunctivitis – in my eyes. It affected my sister's eyes too but she recovered soon. In light vein, she might have had lesser evil or pollution inside her as compared to me. First I neglected the malaise as I was not aware of any such calamity so far in my short life, the disease continued to assume ever more serious proportions by the day. After a week my eyes got totally shut, swollen like balls as those were. Not only that, there was pain as well in the eye balls. Being a child I got alarmed: shall I lose my eyesight? How would then I live? How can one live without eyes? I could then empathise with the blind people.

Nevertheless, there were well-wishers, mostly elder ladies, who had the guts to talk to me in motherly as well as grandmotherly tones to assuage my hurt morale and assure me that it was but nothing to have eyesores, and also, that it was a common phenomenon in those days, rather, in that season in the villages.

My father brought some *'tincture'* to apply in the eyes. An elderly lady suggested that I should be fed brown sugar or jaggery mixed up with *ghee* – the refined butter – as a nutritional cure for eyesores. It was done. Father was both benevolent and enthusiastic those days, particularly, to see his first son grown up as an eleven year old chap. For a young father, having no other prior experience of having one's issues, it is a unique experience to see one's son or daughter reach the lovely age of teenaged adolescence or so. A heart-warming age or shape of a human child!

Not only this, for those were the days of summer season, in our neighbourhood – that is, in the one half of the *Baakhar,* now partitioned as already delineated hereinbefore – there were many a young girl who were favourably disposed towards our mother and happened to converse with our mother and with us, perching on their roof-tops in their leisure time. Those days their another daughter – *Shakuntalaa* - and her husband were in the village, too. Let me clarify here that my divulging her name here is intentional, even as, she was indeed beautiful alike the *Shakuntalaa* of *Kaalee Daas,* i.e. the mother of *Bharat,* the pioneer king of this land of ours -- *Bhaarat.* I confess to be in awe of her unworldly beauty. However averse I tried to remain to the feminine aspect of the Creation, this was a fact that beauty wherever it was present affected me inexorably. I couldn't help it. It used to be spontaneous. Those lady folks were also well intimate with our father and mother, thus spending lot of time at their roof-tops conversing with us. For we were comparatively new to the world and to the village, and also, we were of coming up ages, worth playing with or making mischief with, they had lot of fun with us. During my eye disease of such grave proportions their encouraging words filled my heart with some hope: that I would not lose my eyesight.

One day when I was sitting on my rope-cot perfectly melancholy, not hoping to ever recover from the eye disease, my father came from outside, *Shakuntalaa booaajee* sitting on her roof. Father brought some sugar and *ghee* for me. During conversation, he also mentioned that it was good that I had suffered that eyesore, for once it was cured, there would be no more any eyesore or eye disease for me in near future for years together. I was pleasantly shocked to hear this. I had never heard such a thing by now. By that time I simply had the idea that disease might strike anyone without any cause, and also, that it might not be cured ever in certain cases.

I asked my father in a tone of scepticism, "How is that possible? Why shall I not suffer eye sores in future after this disease?...."

My *buaajee* endorsing, my father expounded to me the nature's mystery, possibly first ever I had come to know, "This is Nature's immutable law that once it has finished the entire filth from within the body, it cannot reproduce the same ill again. The illness is produced due to entry of antigens in the body and the quantity of such antigens is limited. If the protective power of body is able to finish that, it cannot re-emerge."

"Is that so?"

I got amazingly thrilled to come to know of this heartening rule of Nature. I smiled. I added, "Then it's very good! Let entire muck come out of my eyes; I shall be cleansed of the last iota of impurity in this way!"

My father exclaimed in affirmation, even so, my *buaajee* did, sitting on her house, its roof-top.

The sickness was not to last for long; ultimately it subsided, increasing the smile and glow of my countenance, and finally, I was cured of eye disease. My eyes were opened, not only to see the light of the day, but also, to the heart-warming laws of mother Nature. That nothing in the Creation is permanent and forever, everything ultimately comes to an end! Even a seemingly dreadful disease, if proper cause of it is diagnosed and proper treatment is administered taking due care. It was just like

*Buddha's* sermon: cause and effect phenomena of suffering - *Dukkh!* And the path to its annihilation!

I felt thrilled, as if insured against future suffering, that my eyes would not face any eye disease in future, for I had already paid the premium for their insurance in the manner of eyesores. And I should be thankful to my father for this first precept in Natural laws. He was an invaluable soul, too, in so many other respects!

XXX



### 5. *Fancies Ruffled*

*Enter protagonist*

This way from grade six onward I had started living in my paternal village having returned from my maternal grandparents' village – courtesy of the condescension, or of the sense of responsibility felt on the part of my mother's *Jeejaajee,* the husband of her elder sister, towards his *Saalee,* the younger sister of former's wife. In their desolate house which was vacant for last one year or so, that is, after the demise of elder grandma – the *Badee Ammaa*! We, the wretches, did inhabit that desolate and abandoned habitat and made it habitable; they – the owners of the house  - nonetheless maintained all along that they provided us with an indispensable necessity of life, that they facilitated us meeting a compulsory condition for owning an

existence on this planet – an abode, a house, a dwelling unit! In that sense, if they cannot be considered the begetters of our existence, they can safely be dubbed as saviours of our existence, the defenders of our survival on this planet, the planet on which every element of it is supposed to be available free for all, and in ample quantities: the air, the water, the fire, the earth, the space. Whither earth, that's free for all? Every inch of it is claimed to be owned by someone or the other, or is claimed to be the personal property of someone or the other!

This world seems to be in a big mess, or like a big zig-saw puzzle, to start with, i.e. in childhood. One does not have faith on, or confidence in, one's own capabilities and potentials; it does not come as a natural feeling at least. At the time I was admitted to that school the fledgling institution recently initiated at *Inaayatpur* village was merely a High School, that too, only this year having been upgraded from a Middle School. Outside that village, in the east direction, on the edge of a *Pokhar* (puddle), at one end of a very large agricultural field, there were constructed a few rooms with brickwork. Those were not even plastered! At that juncture, those looked absurd as well as haphazard to my child's eyes!

I had returned from *Nanihaal*, the Elysium of my life. At that school, as per my teacher's claim as well as foreboding, I had stood first in the entire area and had topped the Exam Centre. He had announced well in advance of the exam that I would top the Centre; and I did. Or whether it was just that he made us believe like that to keep his prestige intact, I could never know. Yet I feel that this was not a fact; the teacher might have used it as a propaganda, as a publicity stunt, to aggrandise himself, to enhance his importance as a great teacher or a mentor. I feel, too, that all the other teachers, of all the other schools, would just as well have proclaimed like that about the children of their respective schools; that their particular pupil had excelled, or had topped the Centre. That was nothing unusual about my teacher or the other teachers, the academic scenario of the country or society itself being like that: showing off in a sham style, without any qualms of conscience about lying! There was little concern for truth or *Dharma;* the folks were more focussed on prestige; real or false, no matter.

I now remember with a sense of nostalgia, as also, with an equally intensive sense of loss, how high I was pitched on the summit of morale in class five, the fifth standard there! For people, nay, for children, the students, I had become an exemplar! Mathematics -- Arithmetic -- I used to solve all the questions beforehand. There were no difficult questions for me left in the whole book; it was very boring for me not to find any challenge left anymore in the arena of learning. When there are no difficult questions in life, there is no fun as well left in life. No tough nut to be cracked at all!

It so happened that one day *Vinod's* elder cousin, who was himself a teacher somewhere, called me and asked me solutions to many difficult questions in the book of Arithmetic that *Vinod* could not do and had asked his elder cousin, a teacher. I became so hilarious as to become arrogant; I derided him by sort of exclaiming, "Even you don't know, it's astonishing! Then I shan't oblige!" He had felt bad, and he had minced no words in upbraiding me, even as, I was stunned to see his face distorted with contempt, anger and probably smeared with some silent curse. Why did he feel hurt or humiliated? All he said outwardly was, "So much arrogance and conceit is not good for life, *Laalaa* (my dear)! You are acting childishly!"

*Omvatee -- Omaa --* the daughter of our elder maternal uncle, who was almost my age, was standing there incidentally at the moment. I suggested to *Prem*

*Bhaiyaa* - the same *Vinod's* cousin, 'Get it done by *Omaa!*'. But she had already tried and failed. I knew it, and exactly that was the spur for my conceit to misconstrue that I was the reservoir of wisdom in the whole world, leave alone those of my kindly relatives. I intended to spruce up my already shining and high prestige by showing off that even *Omaa* did not know what I knew and could do, and even a teacher of *Prem Bhaiyaa's* stature did not know and could do what I could. *Omaa* too was a very sharp and sprightly girl; as sharp as I was! She was two classes ahead of us in school. But perhaps the maths question was a little more difficult, which my child-brain had somehow solved, and which *Omaa* somehow could not do, which *Vinod* understandably could not do; he could not do even easier sums, how could he? He was the lover of beauties like the unassuming lass *Guddee!* Which even *Prem Bhaiyaa* could not solve, that question I could solve; this feeling was very intoxicating and delusional for the child that I was. And here I was that I wasn't even willing to share my knowledge with anybody! Such a selfish brat! I had probably not yet come across the *Sanskritic* sermon that 'knowledge grows further by sharing the same with others!'

*Omaa* quipped irritatingly losing her patience, "Why don't you tell? You are making such senior elders as *Prem Bhaiyaa* entreat you! Aren't you ashamed? Of your conceit? It's too much! What an accomplishment, that you have done a sum! By sheer chance!" She added mocking me in worst gestures and protruding her sharp tongue.

At this treatment of my giftedness, I felt some guilt conscience. However, my intention was only to publicise my spectacular wisdom, to exhibit that the sums which even the elders and even teachers could not solve I could do. This goal had been accomplished, rather, stretched excessively . Nonetheless, the fruits of the goal seemed probably beginning to sour. Therefore, I solved the question by explaining it to them.

So why was this strong desire for self-publication in my mind? Why was it so dominant in my life? Perhaps the ultimate aim of pursuing education or performing any task in any field of life is self-publicity only! Whither the living creature who doesn't crave his bright shine overwhelming and dazzling the people around him or her!

When I reached the school in *Inaayatpur* holding my father's finger, the school was going to be upgraded to be a High School that year only. A row of some constructed and many a half-built room could be seen standing there. Following my father, I entered the staff room - the teachers' office.

How many childish fantasies were crossing my mind throughout the way from village to the school! I was still in the same hangover: in the fool's paradise of a Centre Topper! In class five, I had topped the entire examination centre, I was told so. I fancied, when my father would disclose about me in the school that I was like this, or that I was like that, the teachers would look towards me with awe and in appreciation! And that the pupils there would clear the way for me, for my arrival – here comes the crown-prince of school *(Vidyaalaya-Shiromani,* nay, *Ashraf-ul-Makhlookaat,* rather)!

But what was this? It turned out to be an anti-climax, rather. I kept sitting on one edge of a wooden bench all alone myself, without even a single glance from anybody having been cast towards me, leave alone from the teachers or the Head Master, the Principal! I felt in my state of dejection that all around there, it was all chaotic as though. Lot of tumultuous activity seemed to be going on there! Everybody seemed rushing around! Nobody whosoever noticed me even for once! Outside, I observed that the boys and girls were making merry, enjoying themselves, indulging in all sorts of mischief-making, and more surprisingly, no one, even teachers who were passing by, were taking any offence to their childish

as well as irreverent hooliganism! They were giggling and screaming, too. In that sense, they were all far advanced and miles ahead of me! I couldn't giggle or coo, nor could I play like them; I couldn't mingle with them in their games.

After a long while, whilst I was sitting morosely there, crest-fallen and with a broken heart, however, a teacher came and finding a kid there, in the staff room, begged with mock severity, "Lad! What are you up to? Why are you sitting here? Why aren't you in your class? Go play outside, or go to your class if it is assembled!"

Then perhaps my father's attention turned towards me, and he interjected, "No matter, he is actually with me. He is yet to be admitted, that's why he is here."

The upbraiding teacher relented and repented as though by chuckling appreciatively towards me.

"Well!"

At the same time, possibly, the Principal got time to take notice of my presence in the staff-room, and he said, "Well, let's write your name!"

I approached him, feeling somewhat irritated, somewhat humiliated. Humiliated, for my fancies had been shattered; also, because I was under the impression that my father was a big gun -- an exclusive B.A. of the whole of area, and also, a teacher of repute at *Jhaajhar* – but here I found to my utter dismay that the Head Master, or the Principal, as they called him, had not paid much or at least immediate attention to his presence. That was however not deliberate, rather, circumstantial, as the Principal was genuinely busy with other people or teachers and had left my father for the ending stretch of his spare time, as was proved, too, when he conversed with my father intimately, as he was free now.

"What's your name?"

*"Arvind Kumar!"*

"Sir, my name is *Arvind Kumar*; it's replied like this!", my father ventured to scold me promptly as was his wont, ever ready to whip out his tongue. My zeal subsided instantaneously, all the sweet dreams, all the fantasies got shattered with this encounter on the first day itself.

'How shall I be able to study in this big school? There in that primary school at *Naglaa Kath* there were only two rooms in all and only two teachers; that too, those two became later, initially there was only one teacher: however very gentle and suave. Here in this *Inaayatpur* school, there were many rooms and many teachers! Everyone had different moods! How would I be able to adjust here? Here there would be much more number of boys and girls; of unknown temperaments and nature! I don't know what type of kids they would be! Everyone would be much smarter and much wiser and more intelligent than I am!' I was lost in these thoughts verging on misgivings when my father interjected: "Come on, bid adieu to Principal *saaheb*! And from tomorrow onward do come here and start studying!"

Then he told something to the Principal in a tone of boasting, "I first contemplated of admitting him to *Jhaajhar* school. In admitting him here, there is a risk in the form of the canal that crosses the way while coming here; that's quite a scare!"

And I was chasing my father once again, this time from school to the village. I could not muster courage even to see my class room. Where would I sit tomorrow? My elder uncle – *Taujee* – and his son, that is, my cousin – *Yuvraaj* – were associated with the same school, *Yuvraaj* studying there whilst the uncle was a teacher there. While returning, we met them in the school, still I didn't have the courage to peek into my room where I had to go from the next day. I was such a shy and effeminate fellow! I rather returned to my home almost holding the finger of my father!

XXX

When I reached the class-room the next day, i.e. the first day of my schooling there, I felt the class as though it were extremely overcrowded. In fact my mind was attuned to the scenario of my last school where there were only a few students. Amidst such a crowded class room I could find no place even to sit anywhere; at least I felt like that. However, one of the boys in the class who looked somewhat of higher age, possibly owing to his stout build and impressive height, offered me some space beside him on the jute strip he was sitting on; and it is this magnanimity or sensitivity of his shown towards me on the very first day that he continued to flaunt as a *cause celebre* for me to be obligated towards him forever in days to come! He could be heard boasting in the class quite often: 'We had offered *Arvind* a place to sit in the class, otherwise he had no place in the class and nobody was letting him in or sit!'

Quite a stuff! Worth laughing at, is it?

The first feeling that crossed my mind in the midst of that crowd was that I could not stand first among all those students; those to me seemed to be very smart, sharp, intelligent and articulate. Awful! All without exception! Look, how they were jumping, hopping and chattering around without any inhibitions or any signs of shyness!

Quite unlike me! Those young souls looked like would-be leaders of the mankind. I forgot all my past achievements – *a la Hanumaan jee*!

'It can't be! It's improbable!', I mused, 'How could it be that amongst all those sprightly and sharp-witted children who looked like the wily leaders at this age itself, I would be the smartest one?'

On the contrary, my father was busy propagating and publicising throughout the village that I would stand first in the class, that I had already stood first in my previous school there in my *Nanihaal* school. Hearing all this bantering on the part of my acknowledged not-so-sensible father, some villagers and the offspring of some of them got overtly jealous towards me. Some even quipped and commented mockingly, even to my face, "Won't be able to come first here, baby! There is already a galaxy of stars here who shine brighter and brighter than you!" Hearing all this from the mouth of a villainous as well as jealous chap I felt utterly depressed and disgusted. My unenvious heart felt an ache.

'Why does he envy me?', I thought. His name was *Naypaal*, literally meaning 'the protector of morals', whither *'Nay'*, the civility? Jealousy for jealousy's sake! 'He is *Anaypaal!*'

Thus, on the very first day of standard six, in the new school, I had lost my self-confidence *a la Arjun, a la Hanumaan*!

'How can I believe that I am the best scholar amongst them all, the most intelligent student amongst them all? These lads and lasses who are so magnanimously endowed by God with such pretty faces, blessed with so sweet and articulate voices, gifted with such impressive demeanour and decency, far superior to mine ones – the inferior one, would they not be possessing a far better and sharper brain than I possess, as a natural corollary?' I was constrained to contemplate like this.

There was yet at least one consolation! A toe-hold, as though! Yet, for me, even that toe-hold was not available. And the solace was that there in this class there was a beauties galore. A multitude of pretty faces of adolescent girls who were attractive and entrancing all without exception, or at least I felt like that at my age of adolescence. That way the disappointment at having missed *Guddee* back there could be abated or attenuated to some extent. However, I had a firm conviction in my mind that it was *Guddee's darshan* (vision, or sight) or it was *Guddee* when she came within my sight that I got spurred extraordinarily, that my brain became superbly charged as well as

energised. Thereafter, however tough a sum or sums I faced, I was able to do them smoothly, without any hitch; the problems that even the grown-ups as well as elders, and even some teachers were unable to solve.

XXX



### 7. *Pre-requisites For Existence*
*Enter protagonist*

*Guddee's* magic remained behind at *Naglaa Kath* with *Guddee*. I came back to my father-land again to study in Class Six. My mother had lived in her *naihar* – parent's house - for a year or more. I was little concerned about what people there did start thinking about my mother and father; that my mother had possibly been abandoned by the 'barbarous man' called her husband. Many a time my *maamaajee* would also call me and make me sit beside him, uttering in front of others, 'I will send him to school till class 10th, then marry him with a beautiful girl: I have already seen and decided such a girl, she would be his age only! I shall mutate 10 *beeghaas* of land in his name; he can till it, grow crops in it, eat, drink and be merry out of it!

That was the time when my mother had only me, one of my sisters, and one baby sister, only three issues. How good it would have been if the father had really abandoned our mother! At least we would not have been victims of poverty! The fallout of my father calling our mother to his village was that there was a queue of children yet to be born. They gave birth to half a dozen children in all! Without thinking about how many crucial aspects of life there were to be fulfilled before begetting issues, and that every child must have a birth right on every such essential aspect of life. But voiceless, ignorant, vulnerable entity is the child! They would not tell it its rights, rather would reel out to it the roster of child's duties on top of that, totally coloured ones! So that it may adore its parents, its teachers, its preceptors etc. as their servant, or it may treat them as gods! So that it may not grudge any injustice done to it! So that it may not scream against the evils and entrenched superstitions of society even when it is hungry!

So that it may not scream against the shiftiness! So that it may not uprise on the issue that when in its case even the first condition of existence – the provision of food – has not been fulfilled, then why should he be made to consider its parents to be worthy of respect! The respect envisaged by mythological *Manu vide* the latter's compendium of mores called *Manu Smriti! Manu Mahaaraaj* would have framed mores and norms as the duties of the parents! Why don't the parents fulfil

all their duties before plunging into the turgid stream of producing babies? Why don't parents venture to beget children only when they have the ability and wherewithal to provide them with proper food to feed, proper clothing to wear, proper accommodation to live in? Proper accommodations, not just pigeon-holes or chicken-holes, the poultry!

The list of duties prescribed with a view to enabling one to command respect from the issues should not end here; there is education, and also, there are other lofty aspects of life, like sports, entertainment, outings, and so on. Only when a couple has the ability and wherewithal to give all this to a person, one should venture to beget issues. After all, it ought to be realised that a baby is not just a pot made out of clay by a potter on his wheel! A child is a conscious being!

If the populace of this country, or of the whole earth, for that matter, is to be brought up to the level of proper sensibility, the arbitrary compendium of codes prescribed for maintaining relations between humanity, parents and the children will have to be torn into pieces and dumped. 'Respect' is something to be earned, to be commanded; it should not be made into a commodity that could be inherited! Likewise, money ought also to be a thing to be earned honestly as well as laboriously, not a thing to be inherited! Exactly this, the tradition of inheriting – the concept of inheritance - has turned the entire social system upside down, reversed it, toppled it, turned it into a hell, perfectly inhumane! This planet, this living universe, this human world! Some people, despite being ineligible, despite being wholly unworthy, even without exerting at all for earning anything, end up getting money, huge money, immense amount of wealth, whilst some people – majority of them – exert to their hilt and try their best to earn money all their lives, yet are unable to avail anything, to afford anything necessary for their existence! How could they? How could one glean the grains from a field from which even the last grain has already been grabbed by the privileged few! First by the rulers, then by the capable (the mafiosi), the remaining lot by *baniyaa-bakkaals* (the merchants and the middlemen)! Whither any residue except the naught, the dust of Mother Earth!

How gullible guys are being fooled! The whole world has been blinded or blind-folded by making them to con the script, by brain-washing them that they ought to follow this rule, follow that rule! That boils down simply to not coming out of the arena of misery, the wretchedness. Whosoever tries or ventures out of this straitjacket blind-fold is pierced by the infallible arrows of violence and torture. Yet the folks are preached that 'violence is sin!' That 'non-violence is a virtue!' Great one! In fact, whither sin, and whither virtue! What is the meaning of the abstract words that have been imposed, they lack meaning, they lack substance!

On top of that, those who have coined and imposed these words, these lexicons, have taken under their command whole of the police force, the whole lot of security forces, the entire contingent of armed forces, as deployed to maintain their own security. As though the security of anyone else, the common people, the folks, is not the responsibility of the army, the security forces or the police! All these groups gathered in the name of public security forces are virtually forced to live in the shadow, in the service, of only those big robbers. Their rules have also been framed in such a way so that they do not use their brains, rather, they do only what they are commanded to do. The result is that they are killing their own siblings, kith and kin, relatives, brothers and sisters, blind-folded. The legacies of the entitled class have been flourishing all the more with the passage of time. Family fiefdoms have become a norm, an incurable disease, an inheritance, rather!

Not that everything was hunky dory as regards the

relationship of our *Naanaajee's* family and the family of *Guddee's* father! In due course, I came across the development in that the congenial relationship had been soured irreparably insofar as the members of our *Naanaajee's* family would not brook any mention of the family of *Guddee's* father. Why such a turn might have come about in such a mysterious fashion in their relations remained a great puzzle for me for quite some time. Nevertheless, when I expressed my astonishment at this development to none other than my own mother she clarified the entire episode to me. She told me that during one mirthful occasion of possibly a wedding at the home *Guddee's* father, our *Naanaajee* happened to pass by that side; he was not invited, incidentally, for the celebratory function, under what considerations I cannot say. Nonetheless, being an influential and seasoned person of the area and being a close acquaintance of that family, when our *Naanaajee* was passing by that side, he thought it fit in his perception that he ought to pay a curtesy visit to the family, if not for anything else. By that token, even his having passed by there without any indulgence would have been interpreted as utter neglect and contempt of the family, implying rudeness on his part.

Yet the father of *Guddee* was not impressed by my maternal grandfather's gesture, under what notion, again, I cannot surmise. He saw the old man looming towards his house and the spot of function, and unmindful of the fact that the sound waves at times traversed long distances quite explicitly and could be heard quite clearly by the onlookers, he commented, "Here comes an old man who is greedy of eating free of cost at functions without even having been invited!"

And the remark reached the ears of the old man so audibly, possibly being carried on the favourable air waves. The old man was shocked beyond limits. He could never have imagined that his acquaintance could make such a mean remark against him and, that too, amidst the company of unknown guests. Practically, his prestige had already been shattered by that remark verging on sheer meanness. My *Naanaajee* was all the more peeved to think that he was being criticized for such a mean activity as partaking of celebratory feast, for which even the strangers were often invited.

For he had reached quite nearby, he could not retrace his feet, and reached the spot, of course, without any sign of rage or displeasure on his countenance. The host – the father of *Guddee* -- too feigned to be welcoming him and invited my *Naanaajee* to have feast, which the latter declined politely. And he left there fairly soon after making a few cursory as well as sham enquiries about the general organisation of the function.

However, unperturbed my maternal grandfather might have been at the spot of action, he could not let go of the issue. Returning home, he proclaimed to his family that such and such was the case, and he ordained that from there onward no truck ought to be kept with the family of *Guddee's* father. And a close acquaintance was lost forever; also, the prospects of my ever having a chance to glance at *Guddee's* bewitching face!

I do not think that my *Naanaajee* was that much greedy for feasts or for free food. Of course, it can't be gainsaid that he was an old man and alike all other old persons he too had developed certain eccentricities which could seem abnormal to the younger generation. It may also be surmised that on any one off occasion or function at our maternal relatives house the feelings of the *Guddee's* father might have been hurt unbeknown to the former; and the latter might have vented his ire against the old man in that fashion. Nothing can be said for certain, however!

Thereafter I never saw that sort of camaraderie between the two families; rather, I never saw them being invited to any functions whatsoever, be those wedding parties or be those the death parties, i.e. the condolence gatherings.

However, this episode immediately launched me on to the memory lane whereby I could visualise so vividly as well as amusingly an incident that had taken place at *Danwar* railway station some time back. In those formative years of my life, when I was not aware of most of the intriguing realities of the human world, and when even the families of my maternal relatives were relatively quite young, such occasions arose quite frequently year after year that one or the other member of the family – be it a son or a daughter – would be getting married, the boys bringing a female member to be added to the family, and the daughters being parcelled off to another's family for good. And unlike these present days, the family functions persisted for months together and guests happened to visit the village quite in advance. To ferry them from the railway station, a bullock cart was sent there and, invariably, we the children would be the drivers for the bullock-cart – *Surendradaa,* me and any other child if at all. At times, any elder member too would like to accompany us, of his own sweet will, even as, that was not imperative that the adults should accompany us. We were supposed to be capable enough to handle the oxen; those were pretty civilized and duly trained unlike humans!

What I intend to narrate is that on one of such occasions our *Naanaajee* himself thought it fit to accompany us to the railway station to receive a particular guest. We reached the railway station as usual, and knowing that the train was yet to arrive and the time gap was almost an hour, we unyoked the bulls and parked the cart beneath the shade of a shady *Neem* tree. To the rear of the platform of the station and the rooms, there were certain huts, in which poor people ran their petty shops. One of such shops was invariably of *Beedee* and tobacco, whereas the other one was, equally invariably and more importantly, that of sweets; sweets not in modern sophisticated sense of the term; those were merely the concoctions of sugar moulded in crude shapes of globules and squares etc. Also some *laddooos* of ground sugar and refined butter – *ghee* – were found there apart, of course, from the *pedaas* – the flat circular shapes of the same stuff. The latter shop had a greater significance for it helped the poor folks purchase some 'sweets' to be presented as gifts to the hosts, thereby salvaging their prestige which was so poorly fragile.

Our particular train was late and meanwhile we opted for perching at the shop of the sweet-seller, toeing the line of our *Naanaajee*. The latter was a well-known respected figure of the area. Who could forbid him from entering the shop, a thatched contrivance only! My maternal grandfather took his place inside the shop, in a dark corner, and beside the *thaalee* -- broader plate -- of *besanee laddoos*, the sweet globules of gram flour. When our old man was perched there how could we the children remain behind! We were nonetheless denied entry into the inner echelons of the shop; we had therefore to contend ourselves with the outer periphery of the shop, that is, the open platform made of simple soil, however, smeared with cow dung paste. Unassumingly, we children sat there hoping that we were waiting for the train's arrival whenever it would. Our *Naanaajee* himself was, nonetheless, sitting comfortably beside the broader plate full of *besanee laddoos*, and queerly with his arms stretched over the *thaalee*, almost touching the *laddoos*.

As far as I am concerned, I observed that queer alignment and wondered how my *Naanaajee* could enter anybody's shop and then sit like that stretching his arms over the plate of *laddoos*. Also, I was wondering why the poor shopkeeper was not objecting to my grandfather sitting like that making his stuff susceptible to theft by him. Instead, the poor shopkeeper seemed to be helpless and was showing excessive respect towards my maternal grandfather using such terms as *'Baabaa!' 'Thaakur Saahab!' et al.* Strength! *Shakti!* Conventional Clout! I immediately realised. It was the clout of a person that ruled the roost, that reigned supreme; no norms, no morality, no legality worked when strength would be at work!

Even as I was wondering why my *Naanaajee* was sitting in that dark corner stretching both his arms over the plate of *laddoos*, I observed that when the poor shopkeeper was engaged with a customer my old man picked up a *laddoo* quite stealthily if unnoticeably, grabbed it in his fist, folded the arm as if he were willing to scratch his mouth and put the laddoo in his mouth and closed it, to be eaten or swallowed very slowly and slowly as if nothing was the matter except natural movement of muscles. When I saw this, my inner righteous child was morally shocked. How could a grown up man of my *Naanaajee's* age resort to such a tactic, that too, for such a trivial thing as a small globule of sweet, such a cheap sweet as was made of sugar and gram flour. I shuddered to think if the shopkeeper noticed the theft what would be to the prestige and honour of my old man! But our old man was unperturbed, rather unconcerned; he had possibly calculated the small

risk. But in my view he was entertaining a grave risk. Whether the other two of my companions observed it or not, I cannot vouch; however, I can only surmise that they might have, still opting to keep quiet as I had done. *Naanaajee* did not stop there; rather, he repeated the feat again, this time using the other arm, and then the first one; and only when he had eaten three *laddoos,* he ventured to leave the shop bidding zealous adieu to the poor shopkeeper. I wondered if the shopkeeper had not noticed what had just happened. I rather thought that the shopkeeper might have noticed the incident as he was a sharp sighted 'shopkeeper', a 'businessman', still he opted for ignoring the innocuous incident for the sake of buying peace, for nothing would have come out of the entire imbroglio had he created one, in view of the trivial stuff at stake and the gargantuan prestige of the landlord at stake thereagainst; nobody would have subscribed to his allegations, he knew it well.

We went to the platform and loitered there for a while, and when the train arrived, we ferried our guests to the *Nanihaal.* However, I was carrying a bizarre experience with me in my child heart, and the carcass of the prestige and morality of my *Naanaajee!* Couldn't he have bought a small quantity of sweets for money if he was so willing to eat them! I kept on contemplating constantly. Then I realised *Buddha's* dictum *'Adinnaa Daanaa Viramani!'* (Stay away from stealing!) But my *Naanaajee* had not come across any such *dhaammik* injunctions in his life, even as, no villagers had ever, too! The rural folks seemed to be guided by their unhindered carnal inclinations only!

XXX



## 8. Benevolence Of Father

*Enter protagonist*

As I have already narrated, my father was scheduled for going to his school for pursuing his *ad hoc* teaching job in a few days. I had been admitted to the school at *Inaayatpur* and had started going along with the other numerous pupils going there, but mostly accompanying my cousin, and quite often even my elder uncle who was an Asstt. Teacher there. Incidentally, all the teachers other than the Head Master, that is, the Principal, were called Assistant Teachers, whereas we pupils hailed one and all as *'Maassaab'* only. My grandfather, however, pronounced the term as *'Maatsaab'*, as was the practice during British *Raaj*.

My father being a scion of feudal set-up and the son of an educated father – of British era – was conscious of the requirements of apparatus and paraphernalia for a student to pursue one's studies in proper manner. He, therefore, got built small-sized chairs and tables for me, which were a novelty in entirety for me. Thus far I was used to studying by sitting on the floor itself – whether dusty or covered with jute strips. Though I did not realise the importance of furniture provided by my benevolent father at that time, I now realise how valuable those gifts were for me! For which, I now feel heartily grateful to my father.

Not only the study table and the chairs, but also, the dictionaries – of variegated sizes and of different languages, both *Hindee* and English – were yet another bounty that my father provided me as a tool for pursuing my studies with higher acumen and efficiency. Those were not the days of Google or Internet or Cloud; one had to depend upon standard dictionaries printed on papers only, for looking up the correct or traditional meanings of the words spoken or to be used in the written texts. Also, for converting the words from one language to the other one!

However, in my childish fancy often I harboured even the notion as if the entire dictionary was supposed to be memorised by heart. All the millions of words therein, and in all the dictionaries! And ironically nobody corrected me in this misconception guiding me in that neither the entire lot of words is required for communicating during one's short life-span, nor is it required that the entire dictionary be memorised. Life in fact can be lived even with the limited stock of words, or stingy vocabulary whatever one possesses, and also, even at the strength of words formulated *de novo* by oneself which can convey the meaning or intention. Furthermore, the gesticulations and bodily hints can substitute for the lack of linguistic words to convey one's sense.

Even as my father had the advantage of his own father being an English educated father, he had, in turn, been facilitated by his father with such facilities, along with the inculcation of feeling that dictionaries and study paraphernalia are very crucial to proper conduct of studies. Moreover, my father was himself a teacher, so to say.

No need to say that he had provided me with sufficient quantity of stationary, notebooks, pens, pencils etc. as well. At least at that initial stage of my schooling I never felt the dearth of requirements for studies.

Food, too, in those initial days was sufficient, for our uncle had provided us one fourth of the produce on the logic that my father was not contributing anything to the cultivation of the landholding whatever he had inherited from his father; it was being cultivated by our uncle only – his elder brother; and in keeping with the practice, he was entitled to keep half the portion of produce unto himself out of our share. For the beginning that seemed to be sufficient quantity for us.

On the issue of sharing of produce, nonetheless, there was much wrangling on the part of my mother with the family of my uncle and aunt. My mother's logic was that for the land was equally shared by her husband and my uncle, the produce must have been shared equally, which logic was entirely illogical. I too in my enthusiasm could not fathom this arithmetic of sharing of produce, and therefore, went to my uncle -- *taaujee*, but to no avail. He and my aunt replied politely that they would explain the entire conundrum to my father. When father came to know of all this, he upbraided my mother sternly in his usual style and commanded that she should have nothing to do with such matters involving males, and that he himself had understood everything well. Nevertheless, he did not take pains or pity to expound the same to us souls endowed with 'lesser wisdom'.

My cousin – *Yuvraaj* – was however a sensible and benevolent soul. His mother instructed *Yuvraaj* to explain the modality of sharing the produce to me and my mother. He did try his best to explain everything, but I doubt we were convinced, I and least of all my mother. Actually, the convictions of both the parties were different. Mother's viewpoint was that inputs being expended on agricultural cultivation were of no consequence, and also, the labour and time invested by my uncle and his family were of little consequence, and that my father and his family even without contributing anything either in respect of inputs or in terms of labour or time were entitled to half the produce for he was the owner of the landholding in equal proportion. When my cousin very politely explained all this to us, he was in fact very sensible and polite, still my mother was not to be convinced, but she had no option. When my cousin left, my mother heaved a deep sigh of aggrievement, "See, how astute they are! Holding half the share of ours for nothing but as a consideration for the marriage of their younger sister, expenses of which they had incurred all alone, your father contributing naught...."

I could not comprehend anything of this familial wrangling. I have reached the conclusion after watching such phenomena over the years that the worst enmity is developed amongst the blood relations only, amongst the siblings only, nobody goes to squabble with the strangers whom they do not know or do not have any truck with. I, in the process, developed a feeling of aversion towards my aunt and my uncle. My mother kept on adding fuel to the fire of angst and enmity, off and on. In that sense, our immediate blood relations had become our mother's worst enemies. We cousins nonetheless remained on good terms. Still, neither the two brothers – my cousins – nor their parents ever visited us at our home, nor did they evince any interest in our activities or our lives. We were miles apart as regards relationships. At that juncture, I felt as if relationships were meant only for developing worst kinds of animosity amongst themselves. At times, I felt that our aunt was the worst kind of lady in the world, as was the intonation given me by my mother continuously. Mother would also add off and on that my aunt had usurped half a kg of gold jewellery that belonged to us. Being a child and all that nonsense coming as it did from the mouth of my mother, I continued to augment my aversion towards my aunt.

However, later in life, I realised that all that was bullshit and that the aunt was strict in demeanour but not that bad or not at all bad. Moreover, even if the alleged jewellery had been shared with my father, that would also have met with the same fate as did all other jewellery or property of the house: everything would have been squandered off definitely. My aunt was as normal a lady as my mother herself was. In fact my mother had her sister as her eldest sister-in-law in the same household. She did not like my aunt's – *taaee*'s -- self-assertive and decent demeanour, and did criticise my aunt as a habit; therefore, my mother too being her younger sister felt duty-bound to criticise my aunt, my *taaee*.

In such a suffocating and inferno type atmosphere where there was no family affiliation, our life started palpitating. Nonetheless, there was no dearth of other households with whom our relations were far more intimate than with our blood relations and they were always at our side in emergencies and exigencies. One such household was *Modhoo chaachaajee's* and his wider joint family, to which, our great great grandma belonged.

Why only this family, the one just in vicinity, that of *Mukhiyaajee* was there and lot many more around. Our front door being towards the wilderness, we were in a sense detached from the village and had a divine opportunity to always face the agricultural fields and their verdure and felt lucky and happy in that sense. That isolation kept us aloof from the general rut of the rural rigmaroles.

XXX


*Enter protagonist*

Having thus established his small family at the shelter house of his elder cousin, my father left for his school at *Veerpuraa*. My father was in an affable mood those days; he had enjoyed company of his long separated spouse. Carnal desires and their satisfaction is a crucial factor in framing a person's immediate behaviour and deciding his mood. Another factor might be that for a short while at least there was no shortage of money being felt in the household, my mother having brought a fairly good amount thereof from her parents' house as the parting gifts.

For seeing my father off I accompanied him up to the town, from where he would pick a bus unto the railway station, from where he would undertake a slow-paced passenger train journey of four stations in between to reach his destination. He would deboard at *Somnaa* station, and from there, the village proper, that is, *Somnaa,* where my father stayed, was not very far. Those were the days of summer or monsoon, so to say. At the bus stop, there were a few shops, rather petty vendors apart from a few trees under which could be sought some semblance of shade and relief from the scorching heat.

On reaching there, my father chatted with me affectionately. That was quite an abnormal behaviour on his part. I had had an impression all along so far, even as, all others around me had given me the impression, that my father was a bad man, a hard-hearted man. I was amazed at my father's soft talk. Maybe he was effused by seeing his eleven year old son, for he was having such an experience for the first time in his life.

He was a known figure in the town and at the bus stop, as I have already mentioned. He was reputed to be belonging to a pedigreed high family of the area. He had been a reputed English teacher at the school in the town. Moreover, he had a nuisance value, too. Nuisance value is the biggest value in a democratic set-up. Even as one might not like to show reverence towards a person, one is obliged to do it if the person is a bully, a mafia, or a person having high nuisance value. People were showing due respect and intimacy towards my father. And I was glad to see all this prestige! Of my father!

In my fancies I then assumed as if my father was the most respected person in the entire cosmos. On top of all the other phenomena of the Creation! How foolish! How childish!

When the bus was about to arrive, I felt that it was good that my father would be away and we would be staying away from him. For his company in any case was ever fraught with dangers of tension as well as un-reasonability. He never let the mind of his dependents at rest. His conduct could not be predicted, too.

Before the bus arrived, my father asked me affectionately, "What would you like to have, *Laalaa* (Dear)?"

I was not used to such offers, nor did I have any clue as to how to answer such offers of courtesy. I therefore replied, "Nothing!"

Father himself suggested, possibly sensing my dilemma, "Would you like to drink Coca-Cola?"

Even as the Coca-Cola was not a big deal for me, and I declined that offer, my father purchased one for me and handed me. I somehow drank it, but its effervescence and the bubbles of gas that emerged from within I could not relish, even as, I was not used to drinking such junk drinks. I had always been used to drinking milk, butter milk and cane juice etc. and to eating the fruits and vegetables. Here it was an alien product intaking which my innards resented. When my father asked me how I liked it, I nodded in affirmation that it was good.

Thereafter the father left. While returning I felt a pang of separation, but soon I reached my shelter home.

We, the kids, were not missing our father; nonetheless, our mother was. She enquired of me what my father offered me at the town, to which, I told that I drank the cold drink. Another *faux pas!* In my overenthusiasm, I added that it was not easy to drink, and to make my point clearer I made my face in jest. I never meant that it was bad, however, my simple mother took it as if I did not like it. That is what communication is all about. As a child how could I fathom such nuances of social communication?

The fallout of that *faux pas* was to be felt next time when my father happened to visit the village after a month and my mother, so as to enjoy the bantering, added that I had not savoured whatever my father had given me to drink last time. In fact I had not been able to tell my mother the name of the drink, as I was not aware of that.

At this, my father felt offended to some extent and somewhat disappointed, and also, mildly aggrieved. He exclaimed, "What? That was Coca-Cola. That is such a tasty drink! Every sensible person relishes it."

Then I realised that I had forsaken the chances for future to get any more soft drinks. A costly *Faux Pas!* However, not that bad, as I have come to realise, of late.

XXX



## 10. Our Well-wishers And Evenings

*Enter protagonist*

With our father gone, and the door of the shelter house being towards the wilderness, or agricultural fields, we were at the mercy of God. The door was a wooden door, merely able to withstand the single stroke of a hammer by a sturdy male or even the first of a strong person. The walls of the house were hardly nine foot high, merely enough to block the outer view; those could not act as the blockade for the scoundrels or thugs or burglars. Anybody could scale those low height brick walls; those brick walls were not even plastered. Therefore, even without availing a ladder, one could clamber up the wall by deftly clinging on to the naked brick corners. The milieu around was not that of saints or civilised populace, too; there were tales galore all-around, of all sorts. Listening to the tales of burglaries, cattle thefts, on the way robberies *et al* it seemed as though we were living in some barbarian region. How difficult it would have been in those distant ages of middle ages when the human society was entirely dependent on loot, marauding and thefts apart from wars? I at times mused. But because our family history was full of tales of valour, and even now they were supposed to be quite influential and resourceful, such risks for us at least were not felt palpably. Still, who could deny the possibility of ever such a danger stalking us in the dead of night! On top of that, my mother was young. And beautiful. Both these virtues are the worst enemies of the possessor of the same!

We, the kids, might not be conscious of these risks, but our elders were, our immediate neighbours were. It had therefore been arranged in the manner that the younger sister of *Modhoo chaachaajee – Deshraanee buaajee –* would sleep at our home along with our family. That would provide a sense of security for the family. Now I realise that with *Deshraanee buaajee* sleeping there, it was like *Raam* and *Lakshman* staying with sage *Vishwaamitra.* The catch was that if *Raam* was there at the hermitage of the sage, the king – the father of the prince – would take all care of its own for the protection of his own sons and the hermitage, which he would possibly never have taken had he been asked to send the armed guards; the armed guards could be lax in their duties in that eventuality. That's why the sage asked for the princes to be sent along with him instead of the army of the king.

If my aunt was sleeping at our home, her family members were obliged to keep a watch on our homestead during the night time and take precaution to protect the same from all such dangers as might stalk a solitary homestead.

This one of our aunts – *Deshraanee buaajee* -- was very affable and benevolent by nature. We felt very pleased in her company. She used to tell us stories daily at night, not only the stories available in the books or folklores, but also, circulating in the area, in the village society. Thus, in this way, we kept abreast of the latest developments and news of the village and area.

Not only the aunt, one more soul visited us daily in the evening hours, that was *Omee. Omee* was the nickname of *Om Prakash* who was the son of one of the barbers of our village. He was a school going lad, of hardly fourteen or fifteen. He visited our household purely as a simpleton. In fact, his father's male residence, the hut, to be precise, was located at a short distance from our house towards the wilderness only. The huts of all the three barbers who were interrelated in fact by blood and had distributed the village households amongst themselves for serving, that is, for cutting the hair and shaving regularly. *Omee* was son of the barbers allotted to our lot. He came from his female homestead which was towards the interior of the village, towards the male residences, after having his evening meals, with the aim of sleeping there with his father and other uncles. On the way, he found our homestead, and with the intention of giving us moral support, as though, he visited us daily. We too felt fearless when we found that we were not alone, that there were others too, to support us in the eventuality of any dread or mishap.

The presence of *Omee's* male residences at a short distance apart from a few more households in that direction only acted as a protective shield for us desolate residents of our shelter home. At least psychologically!

Moreover, there were the houses adjacent to ours on one side, though having their doors on the opposite side. Those were the houses of *Baabaajees*. The people would have been descendants of roaming clans – the *Pravrajits* --who would, in turn, have been the hermits in olden ages. But now they were petty households, indulged in all sorts of worldly chores and evils. They had small holdings and were merely living from hand to mouth.

One might surmise that *Omee* would be visiting us with some ulterior motive concerning our aunt – *Deshraanee buaajee* – who was young at that time. However, that was not true. For our aunt was his aunt as well. Actually, *Omee* visited my mother out of high sense of reverence towards her. My mother hailed from a very rich parentage

and *Omee's* elder brother was married in that area; he knew well that my mother belonged to a very resourceful family in that area. Besides, *Omee's* mother – *Lakshmee* – being a barber's wife was sort of common maidservant for the masters whom her husband served as the family barber. She was a lady of wider contacts and of a cooperative nature, and also, very helpful and cheerful. She had permitted her son to visit us daily to prop up our morale. Rather, when *Omee* did not visit us on any day, we felt alarmed and felt a sense of loss, for he used to reel out interesting stories and news about our area including our village and the town.

As regards the adjacent homesteads of *Baabaajees*, there was a young girl of seductive age; and unfortunately, she was beautiful, too. Their agricultural fields were in the direction where a dissipated young lad's fields were – *Sonpaal's*. He in fact had no qualms of conscience about the sexual misconduct or debauchery even. He rather as though felt it his duty to oblige the beautiful girls, especially, of poor families and of lower castes, by seducing and sexually defiling them. This girl fell as the natural prey to *Sonpaal*. Even at my age, I could sense this phenomenon between the gentle young lass and this devilish lad. Even despite her reluctance, she was helpless in view of the lad's higher strata and upper caste. He was seen frequenting their huts quite regularly, even at odd hours.

It so happened one day in the morning hours, when I was standing at the shop of the milk vendor, yet another *Baabaajee – Baaboo chaachaa* - for fetching milk, I saw the father of the girl coughing alarmingly. In my view, her father did not like *Sonpaal*'s visiting theirs unbidden and unnecessarily. He had the sense and could smell the stench of dubious relationship between the two – his daughter and the brat. The lad was present there at the moment, too. Possibly his presence at theirs in the very morning acted as a catalyst for arousing a bout of coughing in the throat of the old man. In the process, his chest heaved dreadfully, I saw, for these were the summer days and the man's body was bare on top. After some time, before my eyes itself, the poor, wretched, helpless father of the beautiful, helpless, abused girl died. Instead of thinking about the dead man at that moment, I was ruminating about the depravity of *Sonpaal* and about the phenomenon whereby in the society the so-called upper castes and pedigreed people were free to nonchalantly outrage the chastity of the girls of poor and lower caste people. The latter could not even muster courage to protest or resist the lad's overtures.



## 11. *First Murder in* Maar-Haraa

*Enter protagonist*

Our father had left and we had settled in the daily rut of our new life at a new village. At school, I was a non-entity, a dumb and deaf sort of a boy, and unimpressive, with no interest in anything including sports. In the class, too, there was no way to show my worth, for there only the currency of articulate and talkative kids did run. I was definite in my conviction that there I would not stand first in the class, that all the rest would be ranked first, second or third etc. and that I would be ranked quite low, may be the last one; and I had resigned myself to that eventuality. Such was my low level of self-esteem and confidence! And this was despite the fact that I could do every sum of maths and all other homework and classwork quite deftly. Nonetheless, the teachers and the school system had no wherewithal to detect my giftedness out of all the rest, all the chaff. I was considered at the most the same flotsam and jetsam as all the other pupils were.

At home front, of course, at least for the day time, there was the company of my seasoned grandfather, who lived with our elder aunt and elder uncle, his elder son and his family, but had affectionate affiliation with us too. In equal measure as he did for the two sons of our elder uncle and aunt. In a nutshell, we did not feel any sense of insecurity despite living in a house whose front door opened away from the melee of the village folks. This had something to do with our pedigree as well; they were resourceful people; they were strongmen in a sense. Rather, other people dreaded them. Likewise was the case of our relatives at other places where we had relationships.

To cite one such instance, once I had gone to my *Mausee's* – my mother's elder sister's – village. There as a child I noticed to my utter bewilderment that none of the homesteads was locked or even latched. Even the main doors were left azar. The situation was so hilarious that at times even the domestic cattle entered the unguarded house and ate mouthful or to their fill from the sacks of flour and other cereals etc. only to be detected later when the owner of the house returned from the fields and found the cattle sitting comfortably inside the house ruminating. One such typical house was that of my *Mausee* and *Mausaajee*. During my stay, once I had commented off-hand before my *Mausaajee* wondering if it was not risky to leave the houses unprotected and unlocked, or even unlatched in such a manner. My uncle burst into a loud

laughter as was usually not his wont and assured me in a tone of boasting, "Risk? Risk of theft? Here? At ours? ….. Forget! Not even a bird can dare enter this arena… of ours!….."

I was amazed, even as, my chest swell with pride. My relatives were so brave that nobody could dare challenge them, not even thieves and dacoits.

Later on, I realised that they themselves were from the martial race. In a light vein, they themselves were no less than the dacoits!

Almost the same was the scenario at our village. Moreover, being kids, it was not for us to worry about security, safety etc; if at all someone should have worried, it was the mother and also the family elders. We harboured sort of a notion that the village elders all were morally duty bound to protect us from all the dangers of society.

In those days, the flour was prepared at home itself. There used to be grinding stones – hand grind-mill – in every household without exception, on which the village women ground the cereals to convert it into flour. That provided not only the exercise to the bodies of the women, but also, afforded the household the fresh flour to eat on daily basis. Otherwise the good quality flour was susceptible to tiny insects as a natural rule.

We at our shelter house had a hand grind-mill, too. My mother used to get up early in the morning daily and ground the cereals. That was sort of her daily chore and we had become accustomed to that morning stony song. Let me hasten to add that my mother was one of those very few women left in the fast changing society who were still maintaining this healthy practice of grinding the flour on hand-driven stone-mills, otherwise most of the ladies had taken to electric grind-mills for grinding the flour.

One such electric grind-mill was available in our village, too, that was at a tube-well of a wealthy peasant. Apart from providing water to the agricultural fields for rent, the wealthy farmer would also grind the cereals of the villagers for fee, that would be recovered in the shape of a portion of the flour itself. Incidentally, in that process, there were no norms set, and the unscrupulous fellow, or even his assistants, could deduct whatever quantity they liked from the flour thus made. This was not the only misdeed or malpractice they adopted; in the hope of becoming quickly rich or proving themselves to be expedient – cunning, to be true – they most of the times exchanged even the good quality cereals for bad quality ones, and kept the good one for their own and their family's consumption. How far that was

adding to their stock of *akushal kamma* (sins) I can't say, but immediately they appeared to be somewhat well off and happier. For doing all such manoeuvres, they refused to do the grinding in the presence of the customers; rather, they would ask them to come after two or three days, so that they could do the theft in the darkness of night.

That apart, my mother relished her physical exertion in this way. Her family was very small: only a son and two daughters, of which, one was hardly one year old. Another daughter was hardly five. For we had only two rooms of utterly small sizes, rather, both the rooms admeasured equal to a single room, when our mother started the hand grind-mill, it created a sonorous uproar in the house, and in the vicinity in the village. Old ones of the village complained even to the effect that in the serene silence of the wee hours of the morning, the unpleasant sound of the stone grind-mill was disturbing their sleep. Nevertheless, our mother kept on pursuing her daily chore. Also, we felt secure and safe when our mother thus created lot of milling noise in the house. When there was so much noise there was no question of any thief entering the house, we fancied. The truth could nonetheless just be the converse of it.

On one such serene morning, hardly a month after our

arrival at the village, when our mother was busy running her grinding stones, there was an unusual knock at our wooden doors. Mother got alarmed; it had never happened before. But the time was not worth warranting any alarm. It could not be a charlatan or a depraved person who could come to do sexual abuse, nor could it be a thief or burglar or a dacoit; our house was not worth that much. The lady knocking at our door turned out to be our immediate neighbours, the *Baabaajee,* the same lady whose beautiful girl was being troubled and exploited sexually by the village bully, *Sonpaal.* Why she should have come so early, my mother wondered, and asked in awe, "Well, sister?"

"Stop this grinding and making noise!" the lady whispered with a sense of alarm and shock associated with some irritation.

To my gentle mother's enquiring gaze, she further whispered, "*Uday Paal* and his son have been murdered *(Qatl ho gaye hain!).*

*Uday Paal* was the name of my grandfather as well, and my mother got alarmed for a moment, however, recovering soon. In my childish fancy I nonetheless wondered how it could be that there could be another person in the same village whose name was exactly the same as that of my grandfather? It

was only through this incident of murder that I could get rid of the notion that no two persons could have the same name, and also, that the names were inconsequential; they in fact had no absolute value, and were merely a means to identify an entity, be it living or non-living.

The caring lady explained certain other details of the murder including the fact that this was for the first time in the history of human society in our village that a murder of human beings had taken place, and that the father and son *duo* had been murdered, also that the murderer was none other than the nephew of the murdered adult only. She also clarified that the murderer had been nothing short of a crazy and deranged person all along, and that such persons were always dangerous and should have been taken precaution against. Without any inhibitions of shame or morals the lady clarified further that the motive of the murder was sexual affair, that between the wife of the murderer and the murdered adult. The murderer was the nephew of the murdered adult, *Uday Paal.*

Were both father and son having affair with the same lady, the wife of the murderer, their daughter-in-law and sister-in-law, respectively? I mused; but soon came the clarification from the lady herself in that the son was killed in error, for he was sleeping on the rope-cot on which the adult was usually supposed to be sleeping, and the murderer killed him first by striking with a sharpened machete. And when he uncovered his face under the sheet, he found it to be a wrong kill and he proceeded to kill his uncle *Uday Paal* and killed him, too.

Without our asking further, the lady clarified that the murderer was at large, had fled from the village.

There was mayhem in the village. In such a small village, a murder! Humans killed! That too, two at a time! How could a man kill another man? I set off contemplating. The lady departed and offered a sane counsel to our mother not to create noise by running the grinding stones; that was rather the time to mourn, mourn the dastardly deaths of two innocent fellow beings. In dead silence!

That in our village too, where there lived the supposedly influential people like our grandparent and his siblings, a murder could take place was a big shock for my psyche. Many myths got shattered. The village people were ruing the event saying that the village had been shorn of the glory of being a village without any murder so far. Our *khedaa* being the centre of gravity of the village and for the chieftainship – *Mukhiyaagiree* – of the village was with our elders,

most of the post-murder activities took place there only, to which, we children were also unintentional spectators. Many a theory of murder was concocted and circulated. The impact of sexual affair was tried to be attenuated somehow; that was more shocking than the murder proper for the villagers.

But how did they all come to know of it all, whilst the murderer had fled and the abuser had been wiped off?

For the grapevine had it for long: the crazy man had warned multiple times that he would butcher *Uday Paal* for latter's clandestine depravity and incestual overtures with the former's spouse.

The youngest son of the murderer – *Gajraaj* – was my classmate. He was a suave and gentle boy; merely a mediocre. For I was likewise, he had made friends with me. We used to sit together in the class. I came to understand that the murderer was the father of *Gajraaj*. How could it be? How could the father of such a gentle son be a murderer? I also wondered what would happen to the further studies of *Gajraaj*. I was also given to understand that one of the sons, rather, the eldest son of the murderer was an *Aayurvaidic* doctor. Dr *Mahendra Paal* was his name. Very sad! I thought. Now the careers of all of them would be destroyed. If not the careers, at least their social lives would be tarnished for they would now be called the sons of a murderer. However, those turned out to be only my childish concerns emanated out of inexperience. Being the influential people, nothing of the sort happened. They continued their lives as usual and soon came out of the blemish of their father's shadow by ignoring the latter effectively.

The next day or so, or next week or so, when I saw *Gajraaj* in the class, he sitting beside me advised me not to disclose to anybody that he was the son of the same murderer. I was pleasantly shocked, but felt relieved; relieved to think that such a gentle and suave boy would continue his studies without any hindrance created by the incident of this murder. The same boy later on becoming an adult turned out to be equally deranged and crazy.

Also, one day soon thereafter, when we were returning from the school, in that scorching sun, we stumbled upon a bullock cart returning from the town in which there was laden the corpse of one more member of the same family of the murdered ones, the housewife of the eldest son of *Uday Paal*. She had died under the shock of the murder of the young husband of his younger sister, his sister was incidentally the unfortunate wife of the son murdered by mistake. Those in the cart were wailing pathetically.

It was such a pathetic scene! We kids could not withstand that all, chasing the bullock cart as though under spell of death.

The village thus had seen many deaths in cascading order within a week or so. The ill-fate had stalked the family which was a good family by all measures otherwise. I don't know whether the murder was genuinely deserved or committed merely based upon suspicion or craziness of the murderer. Yet sexual affairs are sometimes so sensitive and may turn out to be so fatal, I had learnt even at that age.

XXX



*12. Cauliflower Saplings And The Cattle*

*Enter protagonist*

Having settled at the shelter house in our own village, without our own house, we started watching the developments taking place gradually. I felt constantly that there was vast difference in the life styles and the sense of security between this place and the place of our maternal relatives. Here, we were living in constant scare of petty criminals including the burglars and the sexual offenders. My mother was in her thirties at that juncture. And also, beautiful, attractive! Though the reputation and prestige of the pedigree, the family tree, was very high and sense of awe towards them quite high amongst the inhabitants, there was no guarantee that one's repute or stature in society would ensure immunity from anti-social elements. And there was no dearth of such elements in our bigger establishment, too. There were boozers, depraves and sexual abusers, too. One such person we have already mentioned in the form of *Drig Paal*. Another such scoundrel was *Doongar*.

Nevertheless, to take care of this aspect, and to guard against such scoundrels, there was *Deshraanee buaajee* who would sleep at our home as a psychological support for us toddlers and for our young mother.

The bulk of firewood – the twigs of mango trees – that were procured by our father from the felled orchard, when they had arrived, seemed to be huge, rather, inexhaustible ever. Of course, in our childish fancies! Soon we realised that the seemingly inexhaustible stockpile of firewood had diminished unexpectedly faster, for the passers-by used to pick some twigs and made away with them unbeknown to us.

In the process, however, a portion of the land where the bullock-cartful of load was unloaded had been vacated. When I watched it, I felt like using that attractive patch of land as the agricultural bed for using my skills as I had been doing in my maternal village. I was so fond of growing vegetables, plants and flowers in the agricultural land at my *Nanihaal*!

Those were the days as well as the season when cauliflower plants could be planted. I asked my mother as to what vegetable could be grown in that small bed, and she advised me to be guided by *Omee* in the evening when he visited us as usual. *Omee* not only guided us, but also, procured the saplings of cauliflower from somewhere and made available to us. He might have procured them from the fields that were there on way to town school as I knew. Anyway, I was so glad to have got the cauliflower saplings!

I prepared the agricultural bed well by exerting in making the hard soil cultivable, arable, and worth planting saplings therein. That gave me same sort of satisfaction as I had been deriving in my *Naanee's* village. And the pretty as well as sturdy saplings of cauliflower were planted in aesthetic patterns, that is, geometric patterns. On having achieved that feat so soon after our settling at this new place, I fancied that I could pursue my hobby of gardening here as well, as I did in my *Nanihaal*.

I used to take proper care of the saplings for weeks together, by watering them and weeding them meticulously after returning from the school. In the process, as the nature's bounty, the plants started growing sturdily, and in the proportionate measure my pleasure started taking wings, too. The cauliflower plants, so many in unison, as though singing a song in symphony, or rallying in the field, looked so enchanting! Just like the adolescent lasses! Those at my new school!

At *Nanihaal*, I had never faced the risk of cattle grazing the plants, for the patch of land where I did pursue the hobby of gardening – rather, miniatured farming -- was duly segregated and isolated, unto which there was no approach of cattle. And in the process, I could not develop the sense of risk associated therewith. Here, as a protective fence I had erected a fence of tender twigs around the cauliflower bed, and by doing so, I assumed in my mind that I had taken every care to ward off the wayward cattle. This was however not in conformity with the reality of the Creation; the cattle could not be checked from grazing one's crop by such simple measures. The fence I had put up was nothing for the cattle.

However, one afternoon, when I returned from the school, and when I was expecting to relish the beauty and greenery of my cauliflower bed, I noticed to my utter dismay and horror that there was no cauliflower plant anymore in the bed; it was vacant alike a barren land. I felt crest-fallen. I rushed to my mother throwing the school satchel helter-skelter, and demanded, "Where are my saplings?...of cauliflower?....."

"I don't know. What happened to them?" my mother rushed to the front of the house where the cauliflower bed was supposed to be. She was shocked, too. Genuinely so.

But I was shocked as if my children had been butchered. "How pretty those looked! How attractive! And how sturdy they were! We were expecting them to bear fruits soon!..." I was wailing with deep emotions. My emotions were no less than I would have had for the death of my kids, my own issues. Attachment! I was inconsolable.

"Someone – my enemy – has done it! Deliberately! I tell you!" I was blubbering.

"No, who would do it? This is the doing of cattle." My mother tried to console me and assuage my soul.

That was logical but in my childish fancies I could not imagine that any cattle could come all the way to our gate and graze every piece of sapling from my bed which I had cultivated so fondly and so laboriously. I had fallen in love with them.

That was a big shocking episode for me at this new shelter. For me the child of hardly eleven. I was not aware by then that so many multifarious and much graver setbacks were in the offing yet to come in my entire life.

In the evening, *Omee* and *Deshraanee booaajee* too contributed to the efforts of my kind mother to assuage my aggrieved heart. They agreed on one prospect at least that it was the handiwork of cattle, not of any human species, the supposed enemy. To this I nevertheless upbraided my mother as to what she was doing when the stray cattle came and destroyed my entire crop?

"I could not notice." My mother replied.

"That's very careless of you, *Beebee!*" I wailed again. I addressed my mother as *Beebee,* incidentally, implying a sister of her brothers.

"We shall bring you another bunch of saplings that you may plant again," added *Omee,* merely to assuage me. My mother nonetheless added that the cattle would not leave the plants un-grazed; that they would come again and destroy them once again like this only.

And I resigned to my fate: and decided never to undertake the hobby of gardening or agricultural pursuits in my paternal village! That was the wont of all the male populace in the broader family set-up, and I by the hand of Providence had been thrown into that band of indolent people. The Providence came unnoticed in the shape of cattle and grazed my industriousness and soft feelings, the child's innocence.

XXX



## 13. Drawing A Cow On The Wall Of The Room

*Enter protagonist*

Ours was a small house, as already declared hereinbefore. To maintain such a small unit was very easy as well as comforting, too. Family, too, of my parents by that time was very small: hardly me, my sister and one baby sister – the latter I did not notice, however, that there was one. The youngest sister I did notice only after a year when my mother had been to *Ajmer,* to her sister's and when she returned she came back with a very pretty child seeing whom at the first sight I was bewitched. A two year old kid!

'Such a fairy in our wretched house?' I thought.

"Who is she?" I enquired of my mother who had just returned from her sister's home at *Ajmer*.

As though befuddled, my mother replied in mirth, as was her wont, "She is your sister, don't you know?"

"Where did you get her?" I asked again in amazement, for I had never noticed such a thing of beauty in our household earlier.

"She was already there when I left here, as a small baby, can't you recall?"

"But it was not so beautiful!"

My mother laughed plentifully and whole-heartedly, and added, "Yes, she is beautiful, very beautiful! Do you like it?"

I nodded in affirmation. And was extremely effusive. The exceptional beauty of that child filled me with the sense that we were very fortunate to have such a beautiful child in our midst. My mother was bemused.

It was nothing for our father; he had no sense of beauty or ugliness, for that matter. It was nothing for my mother either, for she was grown up enough to have the knowledge that all the children at the age of two or three look equally attractive, innocent and enchanting. By grace of God. The grace of creator is reflected through their countenance.

I took the small toddler onto my lap and took it outdoors, to the village, as if to declare to the world, the society, that we were not poor vis-a-vis others as we had a beautiful sister in our household. I knew that we were extremely poor people as regards food, clothing and housing, yet with the coming of that beautiful creature, I at least felt that we were rich in terms of beauty.

However, I was discussing my school days. At school, we were taught the 'drawing' as well. One day it so happened that I chanced upon a piece of paper lying somewhere, upon which, there was printed a lovely cow with robust bestial body. I was mesmerised by her beauty. I picked the picture and brought it home. In the process, somewhere it occurred to me on reaching my tiny room – whose walls were not yet white-washed but plastered – that I should draw the similar picture of the cow on the wall above the niche on the facing wall. This thought occurred to my cerebrum that I was an exceptionally brilliant student and I should have the skills to draw exceptionally well, too. Also, that the moment I would draw the cow on the wall of my room, the people of the family would praise me no end, and I would prove myself worthy of that praise.

I set off drawing the cow on the room's wall forthwith. Soon I realised that it was not as simple as it seemed to me initially. Still, I persisted, for I had already pronounced to my mother boastfully, and she had nodded to my artistic project; how could I now backtrack! That was a question of prestige for me. Within a week or so, exerting a lot, standing on a wooden table, and using the eraser multiple times, I could draw the cow ultimately and derived satisfaction of having achieved something I had resolved to do. The pleasure of having accomplished the resolved aim is unique indeed!

The 'drawing' did not turn out to be a perfect piece of art; its rear portion was awkward and disproportionate, let me confess, yet I contented myself by that much. That much deficiency would do for a child like me, I assumed. Moreover, in real life, I had seen many cows having such deformities as were depicted unintentionally in my drawing!

My mother praised it, I know, merely to encourage me; my *booaajee – Deshraanee –* praised me genuinely, for she said that it was not easy to draw a cow on a wall like the one I had done so dexterously. *Omee* applauded it to give a boost to my morale, and *Modhoo chaachaajee* praised it, too, even as modestly, or as a matter of modesty. And I started taking myself as a great artist, who could draw alike the portrait of *Mona Lisa.*

In the process, I realised that if one decided to achieve something one definitely could. I had no prior experience of drawing a cow or any cattle even on paper.

To see that his lovely and dear daughter was settled well at her shelter house, my *Naanaajee* happened to pay a visit to our refuge shelter. When the cow drawn by me on the wall was exhibited to him, he was so appreciative of it! He over praised it and I then felt assured that when such an adult as my maternal grandfather was praising it whole-heartedly, it must be a genuine praise, and that I was *de facto* a great artist there-onwards.

Nonetheless, not everybody was that sensitive as my mother or *Naanaajee* or other well-wishers of ours were. A long time thereafter, when I had resigned to the idea that my cow was an exquisite piece of art, there came the visit of our saviours from *Ajmer*, that is, the eldest daughter of our patrons visited the house – their house. Along with her younger brother, the latter of my age almost, maybe somewhat older. When with utter enthusiasm and with the expectation that they would appreciate, too, my child's efforts in drawing the picture of cow, that too, on a wall, standing on the table while drawing, they callously laughed and derided my artwork commenting that the rear of the cow was out of proportion. I knew it was, yet I expected them to be sensitive enough to appreciate my artwork. Her younger brother was all the more insensitive, foolish, even as, he was more scathing in his comments. I was not amused. I developed a dislike for them somewhere in my heart since then. An aversion for those urbanites!

Living in the city, in vulgar surroundings they had lost all sense of decency, sensitivity and sentimentality, I concluded.

Thereafter, the cow had lost its significance for me, though it remained there for long. I once asked my mother to wipe it off but she did not permit me to do so. For her, it was a *Mona Lisa,* an exceptional piece of art work done by a piece of her own heart. She did not let it be wiped off even when once we whitewashed the walls. That particular portion where the legendary cow was drawn was left untouched.

For a mother it mattered everything! For me, too, my mother already was, and became thereafter all the more everything!

XXX



## *11. Perfect Prescience*

*Enter protagonist*

This was the question paper of *Hindee* and the examination was the First Terminal Examination, that is, the one held after expiry of three months after opening of the school. I had always been very fond of question papers, those crisp pieces of parchment on which were printed the questions to be answered during the exam. Exams had never scared me whereas all other beings considered exams or tests as an ever dreadful a phenomenon. Thus far in my schooling life, I had never been lucky enough to get printed question papers in barring a few ignorable exceptions possibly! The exam fees having been collected from the pupils religiously, notwithstanding! Nevertheless, the teachers fulfilled the rigmarole or ritual of holding examinations by dictating the question papers by word of mouth or simply by chalking them down on the black boards. This time my heart felt a sense of pride and my mind felt very pleased to hold the crisp and glazed 'printed' question papers in my small hands. I was feeling an other-worldly and unforgettable excitement at this otherwise not-so-remarkable a development. I fail to fathom this mystery. This can be fathomed by only my body and mind, how can I know all about these puzzles? In this mysteriously secret cave of my physique, or you may also say, in the cavern of my physical body, I feel, I am merely a hapless and helpless body-passenger! Who is obliged to stay on board it notwithstanding its physical and mental condition!

Why was my psyche so excited at getting the question paper, such a trifling thing? Wasn't I crazy or a buffoon?

I was so obsessed with the smoothness and crispiness of the paper that I did not let even a single crease pass on to it. Not a single mutilation or dog ear I could tolerate on the smooth paper. I took the paper as such, unmutilated, unsoiled, to my village, to my home. I was constantly cautious that nobody should touch the paper with one's dirty hands, that nobody should mould the paper and create any crease on it; and I did not let anybody touch that piece of unblemished parchment.

Nonetheless, all along the lengthy distance of almost two kilometres, I was engrossed in the task of evaluating my performance in the exam in that first paper. Finally, the mind agreed on one number – 34 -- . When I felt satisfied, doubly convinced that I would not secure more than that, I wrote 34/50 with a raw pencil on the paper itself using the 50 already written against maximum marks. This I wrote very beautifully, so as not to soil or spoil the artificial grace of the paper. It is only after several decades of life having been lived that I have now reached the firm conviction that there is something veritable called 'intuition'. In the stages long after my life's journey, I have come to know that there is something called 'intuition': very powerful and indeed true. Later on, it transpired that it was exactly 34 that I had scored in that paper when the answer-sheets were displayed to the students.

However, I reached home. I was not enthused; as I thought, the performance was not up to my mark, not commensurate with my potential and my expectations. I harboured a misgiving that other students could secure much higher scores in the paper. I felt as though I had plucked in the first paper itself; how could I excel in the rest? After the mark of 34, there were 16 milestones, goal posts, 16 chances of defeat, 16 probabilities of lagging behind in excellence, I mused in my childishness. That there might be 16 more students in the class who could be wiser than I was, by virtue of occupying those 16 slots that were left unoccupied by me.

Nevertheless, when I had had my food in that morose mood only, despite my mother's expressing hope and enthusing me, one of my uncles – *Modhoo chaachaajee* – happened to visit us hailing *'Bhaabhee! Bhaabhee!'* Readers might recall, he was the same benefactor of ours who had brought us from *Nanihaal* at the beginning of that year; also, the readers might recall that he was very fond of scaring the kids and toddlers including me. It also maybe that the perverse action of scaring their children was the easiest excuse to make contact with sisters-in-law, the *Bhaabhees,* especially, prettier ones, the attractive ones. What else was there to converse, to find as an excuse?

My mother was concerned – and genuinely so -- about my

education and its standard, given that so far I had been a prodigy and a force to reckon with in my previous schools. She wanted to ascertain whether here too I was on the same track, or here, there were other worthies who could excel far better than I did. She had in fact sent for the uncle a while ago. And I presented myself in the court of my uncle with a shiver in my heart about my perceived mediocre performance in the paper. The performance was evaluated. Mother was blank about such matters: what *Hindee,* what Maths, or what English was? She was an absolutely illiterate as well as unlettered lady. Whatever little knowledge she possessed about the alphabet of *Hindee*, by now she had lost that property as well. The uncle made me to revise and solve the entire question paper once again, and remarked enthusiastically, "You have done marvellously well in the paper! Bravo! You will score 34 marks!" He also added, "34 in *Hindee* is a very good score!"

I was nonetheless not enthused. I pondered, rather, 'What sort of *Chaachaa* he is? 34 marks, and he says, it's a stellar performance! Whither congruity in these two facts?' However, it was to dawn upon me only later on that 34 marks in *Hindee* was really a stellar performance and that it was me alone in the entire class who had secured way ahead of all others;

others having secured only below 20 or so.

I took the whole gamut of exam like that only, without self-confidence and *sans* any great enthusiasm. I was dead sure that here in this school I was not going to top the class, leave alone the school. I had no aspiration, too, that I must stand first. For the heart and mind had forsaken the desires and aspirations, they were in a state of perfect calm and quietude. Otherwise, when I used to place myself in the mad race of competition and on the pinnacle of performance, I was always upset and under extreme mental stress.

Then came the day when the answer-sheets were returned to the students after evaluation for perusal by the latter. It was the same *Hindee* answer-sheet that was shown first of all; and I saw to my extreme amazement and with an admixture of pleasure and disappointment that it was exactly that magical number of 34. As if it was the personification of my prescience, of my truthfulness, of my intuition. Had I envisaged bit higher, I would have secured still higher, I contemplated bemusingly. Why disappointment then? For I had not secured more than what I had envisaged! Humans expect ever more than what they deserve or what they would get commensurate with their performance and skills.

The desire to hold on to the truth is really strong in childhood. It is perhaps easier to prescience the future, the unknown, the unforeseen, by way of fore-sightedness. Perhaps that is why I came to guess perfectly as well as correctly the marks I would secure in various of my question papers during the quarterly examination, immediately after writing the exam in that particular paper.

By this time, until this first quarterly exam, I was an unknown face, an unassuming personality, entirely faceless, least spoken, absorbed in myself, in a sense a lad preferring to catch the finger of others or elders. Rather, absolutely lacking any identity. No one knew me, nor did anyone desire to know or talk to me except *Dharmapaal*, the same guy who had been my chum at the town school in basic classes, and who had made me aware of the tale of *Raam* for the first time in my town school.

XXX



*15. Catapulted Into The Orbit Of Fame And Fairies*
*Enter protagonist*

The old *shaastras* hold it that fame or prestige of a person comes handy and works as a protective shield if one is caught in difficulties at far off places. Till I came across this *shaastric* injunction I used to feel all along that the fame was a big nuisance for the one who had incidentally to don it, or suffer it. Weird thinking! Yet my conviction was formulated in the wake of my having been catapulted into the highest orbit of fame immediately after the showing of marks in the first quarterly exam. Whatever tranquillity and peace of mind I could enjoy here at this village school was merely for three months, and thereafter there was no respite. Fame! Such a coveted possession! Craved by one and all! Instead, I found it quite destabilising, even as, at subconscious level I might be relishing it.

When the marks of the quarterly examination started pouring in, the mist on my heart started evaporating, too, in that I had no identity thus far in my school. As the numbers came, my glorious stature started taking shape. I became a hero in the eyes of the people, the teachers and the classmates, irrespective of whether I wished it or not. A virtual or provisional hero - because the quarterly examination had no lasting significance. Therefore, *mahaarathees* like *Dharmapaal* got only jealous, and pledged, in turn, to stop this little rabbit – me - from vaulting forward.

Nonetheless, whilst the fire of envy was raging in the minds of boys, I could perceive that the eyes in the camp of girls, the adolescent lasses, were beginning to rise and look towards me. There were many a such face that did not count me in any category prior to that, and maybe somewhere in my heart I regretted that, too. After the exam results, I found myself in a perfectly different orbit hallowed with a different identity. All those fairies started looking at me with sweet smiles and affection, if only not with romance or love.

I thought, I had won the *swayamvar* – the competition to win the brides - not one, but all the teenaged girls had as though become my own, very personal! *Raajeshwaree* was on top in that group, as far as my implicit liking was concerned!

*Raajeshwaree!* Who shook me out of my drowsiness – the indifference towards her and the other beauties – the other day on way to my school from village, by hailing me from that hump of soil: *'Arvind!'*. I didn't like that any girl should have loved me, or least of all, should have called me so openly, so brazenly and so unabashedly. Yes, paradoxically, I also wished somewhere within my heart that those teenagers loved me, liked me, however, only clandestinely in their heart, without informing me, without disclosing it to others, to the society, to the outside world. That thought filled my inner self and brain with enthusiasm, inspiration

and super-consciousness – so as to do something extraordinary, to score even higher, even more marks.

Until then I had possibly not come across the dictum in vogue in English world: 'Show the one you love that you love him or her' or 'if you love someone tell it!'

XXX



*10. Boon From The Goddess Of Wisdom:*
*Enter protagonist*

In childhood, the speed of time is very slow! Every month passes like a year! The passing of a year gives the feeling of an aeon having elapsed. It was only four months back that I had left class five, but whenever a reference was made towards that period, it felt like 'a year ago'. With every remembrance or memory in that behalf we prefixed it with 'in class five' or 'during last year'. We seldom used or felt like using the term 'four months back'.

Similarly, four months of the new school also seemed like the passage of four years. Time passing at a slow pace one second at a time, one minute at a time, thereby metamorphosing itself into passing of hours and days! It felt as if the school curriculum, i.e. the course, was extremely brief and the time at our disposal far more than enough! Therefore, the sports started to take a lion's share in the stock of our time. That was accompanied by lots of rumblings, squabbles and quarrels with fellow playmates at the village. The boys who were lagging behind me in respect of the power of brain power would try their best all the time to put me down in respect of sports. I was very much allergic to fights or conflicts; it seemed that if I indulged in fight of any kind with someone, my life would be wasted, or that I would forfeit the right to salvation, the *moksha!* My mother had given me strict instructions to go straight to the school, proverbially, in the direction of nose, and come home straight, too – not straying around.

Nevertheless, I felt that even without wandering around, even while walking on straight paths, there was no respite, no question of me walking peacefully. It was not rare that on some days some nagging creature, in fact a boy or a girl, would come and harass me - on some pretext or the other. I assumed that those lads were jealous of me. One of them was also a very intelligent girl whose physical assets were very rich. At the time the marks were being told, she felt stung to see herself lagging behind me. She had never before considered me worthy of her attention or interaction. I wasn't even worthy of her, that's a veritable fact: she was also somewhat stout-bodied. When she lagged behind me even in a

subject like English, in which she thought she had an entitlement to score over me due to her pedigree and upbringing, she suddenly got palpably irritated. Nonetheless, she had turned her anger into love before her angst against me could approach her lips in the shape of something contemptuous against my brightness. She rather uttered, "Why O lad! What have you written in the answer-sheets that you are getting the highest marks, that too, so highly?"

Her cheeks had turned pink by the time she could complete her sentence; she was blushing profusely, I observed vividly. 'Blushing' what they call in English! That divinely beautiful girl as though surrendered to me unarmed! I was taken aback and felt perplexed to find her suddenly speak to me like that. I had never imagined or even aspired that such a beauty that resembled *Urvashee* of mythological fame should ever condescend to let me hear her sweet voice, that too, full of love and affection towards me. Yet the feeling that she was vanquished and felt frustrated disturbed my mind. Nonetheless, how was I at fault in that I had scored higher than she, or the highest in the whole class?

However, some mediocre type boys, who were fond of considering and calling themselves *'daadaas'* of the class even started saying, 'He is in fact the son of a master, a teacher, so he has been given more marks by the teachers! Fraternal bonding! There is rigging of exams and prevalence of nepotism everywhere in this world!'

But *Shaaradaa* – I can remember her name; by penetrating the thin layer of the consciousness, perhaps the computer of my heart has searched the name of that undeclared beloved of mine, the unflinching admirer of mine – from my memory – but *Shaaradaa* too was the daughter of a teacher only! Those rabble-rouser sort of lads came around when she was gossiping with me and set off reeling out the untold tale of *Shaaradaa* to me unbidden, "Her father is a Head Master, too, in an Inter College somewhere. He will take her with him sooner or later; he will not let her remain here, in this rural school. She is very intelligent and gifted. Why would she be left here, to study in these rustic environs?"

I felt hurt to hear all this bantering, if only this was all a loose talk. I was the brightest boy empirically and a proven one! Yet I did not have any other means to study somewhere else! In some prestigious place or school of repute! Except for this rural school! The father of that beauty was a Head Master somewhere in some school; he might take *Shaaradaa* away sooner or later, but take away he shall definitely. He can give her a good education by admitting her to some better school. And she may stand first there, too, in that school! For, the far superior and more intelligent pupils would be left behind here in these rustic as well as dusty environs to accumulate dust on their glitter and wisdom while studying in these so-called rustic schools! For these unmatched prodigies there is no other place anywhere on this planet!

Nevertheless, pure and hundred percent pure gold does not qualify for making jewellery of any sort! The value – the price – even if it be that of one's intelligence or wisdom – for being appraised optimally takes commodification in tradeable form! It is only the trader's wares that fetch optimal value or more than that. Others get the price of brass even for their golden wares!

*Shaardaa's* sympathetic and desperate voice made her sympathisers my unprovoked enemies. She was the Principal's daughter. She was endowed with beautiful body and an enamouring countenance, also with an enviable health; and now the chaps – her admirers – did proclaim that she was also intelligent. So should I have hidden my glow simply for this reason? Be that as it may, I began to dread my shine, my glow, my fame. My praise, my admiration, my fame, began to haunt me constantly. I felt insecure in front of *Shaardaa,* the privileged prodigy.

But it was she only who broke my silence; she chuckled and added, "Thou art really gifted and smart, *Eh!* God will gift you with even more intense intelligence! These are my wishes and blessing for you!" I was stunned to hear this coming as it did from the lips of the most gifted girl of our clan of classmates. *Shaaradaa's* boon! *Saraswatee's* boon! The blessings of the goddess of wisdom and letters!

And on the third day after this solo interaction with that beauty, my eyes were looking for her! I was overwhelmed by sorrow and felt a sense of loss to hear from those urchins of the class that *Shaardaa* had left for *May-Raastra* (called *Meerut)* along with her father, to pursue better studies there, and never to be seen here again! Amidst us vulgar lads!

XXX



## *17. Sham Superiority*

*Enter protagonist*

*Shaardaa's* departure from my school shocked my child's sentiments. That beautiful, lovely faced girl, whose sweet voice I did not even imagine to hear in my dreams, not to speak of wishing to hear ever, eventually, when she chose to speak to me to make me privy to her melodious voice, it was

on her last day in the school; and then she went away for good, leaving the entire scope of excellence in academics for my sake. There was no competitor left for me anymore. There was no *mahaarathee* left in the battlefield of *Vidyaa* - the learning - in front of me so as to compete or challenge me anymore!

Nevertheless, what kept on nagging me ever more thereafter was the thought that I was so unfortunate. How unfortunate I was not to get better opportunities and better options of schooling as *Shaaradaa* could get! I mused. I was more intelligent and far gifted than *Shaaradaa* was, yet I had to content myself with pursuing my studies at this ramshackle school in this rural area which my co-educationists derisively dubbed as all but 'substandard'! Whilst *Shaaradaa* had been blessed by God or facilitated by human society to pursue her studies at a better school, and also, at a luxurious place, like, a city, the urbanite environs. Definitely, she would overtake me if only not in the context of brain power, but certainly in the context of prestige and glitter, for here in this rustic environ, I shall be collecting dust on my brain power and performance, however sparkling might be my lustre. The urchins here in this school – my classmates – aren't even willing to accept that any gifted chap might study in such a rustic school as this one, that too, in this village. There was therefore no question of brilliant scholars getting produced by the instrumentality of such a third rated school located in such rustic milieu!

However unglamourous might be the circumstances, I had no such facility as to go away from home and stay in a town or city and pursue my studies there in conducive and encouraging environs. The urban areas by that time to me appeared like the divine spheres where only the blessed ones could dwell. Glittering with electric lights and provided with all sorts of comforts and luxuries! I harboured a notion that all those who dwelt in cities would be *sans* any sorrows and would rather be endowed with providential pleasures; that all its inhabitants must be well-clad and tidily dressed! Also, that there would be no dust or dirt found around anywhere in the urbanite environs!

My grandfather was an unemployed person. His father and grandfather were wealthy farmers, too; they were landlords, so to say. They had a status, a lot! There used to be *'khaandaans'* - pedigrees. They belonged to one such pedigree. They were called *'Maar-hare Walon Kaa Khaandaan'* or *'Mar-hare Wale'*. They had relationships within the same sort of strata, of rich and prosperous people, people with prestige and status – all the 'high families'. Without exception!

Now that the scenario has undergone drastic change: new actors have descended onto the stage of the veritable theatre called human society, for making a sense, those *khaandaans* - the family fiefdoms - were akin to present day schools, parliaments, local goons, mafiosi, political leaders *et al.* Their lifestyles or philosophy of life was dependent on pressure tactics, exploitation, torture, un-sentimentality, and on top of all, the sham showing off, that is, conceit. The heads or *pradhaans* of villages were all dependent on the wielding of power, ruthless power; even today they are.

In the self-aggrandising and conceited background of those times, those who were fortunate to be born in such families by chance of Providence considered themselves to be the favourites or beloved creatures of God – privileged ones. And why shouldn't they have? The social set up is formulated astutely or cunningly like that – deliberately, just like a game of gambling, by the wily ones of society! Living amongst society is nothing short of indulging willy-nilly in the game of gambling as though. One who somehow contrives and succeeds to hoard money from society, by hook or by crook, by deceit or by conceit, by force or through ransom, by muscle power or by mental manoeuvres, by fraud or through scams, rarely has to worry about earning money thereafter: money does come to such an unscrupulous *homo sapiens* unbidden, unasked for, itself it keeps on coming to him. To even one's progenies, the succeeding generations, after one dies! Irrespective of whether one's progenies be illiterate, unlettered, uneducated or unworthy! One who got born to such rich parents or family fiefdoms was blessed forever, rather, perennially! One does not at least have to worry about earning something as trivial as money. One has not to bow down or stoop to any entity for earning such a despicable thing as money!

How pathetic it is that the divine creation, like, human being, has to struggle throughout one's life and die unsatisfied, running after this earthly *maayaa*, this wizardry, this man-made deception, this mirage of the phenomenon called 'money'! How many of them get the opportunity to move towards or pursue the real goals of life, to practise and attain the sublime ideals! Most of the people find themselves simply trapped in the vicious cycle of fulfilling the basic needs of the existence, of this carnal body!

XXX



18. *The Bullies Due Died*
*Enter protagonist*

At *Inaayatpur* school, it was not all hunky dory for me. I being the soft-spoken and soft-skinned handsome boy, I was the stuff for ill-mannered girls and boys for teasing and torturing in the class. And the number of such rascals was not few.

Also, there were lads who were rash in behaviour but they seldom gave me that much importance as to consider me worth troubling by them. Out of so many multi-mannered lads and lasses in my class, there was one abrasive sort of lad called *'Shree Krishna'*. He was strong-bodied, unlike me and unlike most of the class-fellows. He was rude, as I and many others in the class vouched constantly. He did not like to talk to the class fellows on equal footing. In fact, he was the son of the person under whose aegis the school was established and was still being run. He was sort of a *Chaudhary* (the headman, the chieftain) of the village. Most people might not like this appellation to be used for him though! The noble lady named *Kelaa Devee* who had established this school on the estate or agricultural land of her deceased father, who had left no surviving son, was the sister of this *Chaudhary* of the village. That feeling of *Chaudharaahat* might be working on the psyche of the innocent boy in having nurtured that sort of abrasive behaviour towards his fellow colleagues, or classmates.

I dreaded him, therefore, I seldom ventured, of my own, to talk to him. I was small-bodied and a coward child, full of inferiority complexes, due to the un-peaceful atmosphere of my home due, in turn, to the irascibility as well as short-temperedness of my father. I kept on wondering those days how it was that so many types of human beings had been created by the God Almighty on the same planet, which has similar endowments for one and all in the form of *Panch Mahaabhoots, viz;* earth, air, water, fire and sky.

When I eventually excelled in the academic performance at the school, I feared that *Shree Krishna,* out of malice and envy towards me, would start troubling me, even as, many other rascals had already started doing that. In reality, nothing of the sort happened on the part of the perceptibly rude bully; and the matter of fact is that he was quite polite with me in his behaviour. Nonetheless, he had quarrelled with so many classmates even within that short span of two or three months of the opening of the session, or our joining the school in class sixth.

One day, when we reached the school, it was declared that the school would be closed for the day, for *Shree Krishna* had died by drowning in the canal flowing nearby. The same canal that I have mentioned heretofore, that fell on the way from our village. A sad news indeed, nonetheless, I felt no sorrow, to be true. At that young age, I could not realise the agony of the parents of the lad as to how painful and unbearable it would have been for them for the rest of their lives. He was their only son, rather, the only issue. Moreover, he was the son of the *de facto* proprietor of the school. The teachers of the school were, therefore, duty-bound to attend to the mourning formalities of the young boy, even as, he was the student of our school.

Somehow, in my heart I, and other gullible chaps also in their hearts, felt that a big nuisance had been wiped off our psyche, that it was a good riddance. Since *Shree Krishna* would not be there any more, there would be no more strife and ruckus in the class. And that I would be free from the fear of getting upbraided by that bully.

Now, at this far distance in time from that moment, I feel how ignorant I was. I had lost a fellow human being, a young creature, alike me only. There is none here on this planet who is not ours; also, there is no one here who is ours! All are living their own lives in this rigmarole of Creation.

As all the mortals are ultimately forgotten, *Shree Krishna,* too was forgotten! Wiped off our memories!

During the same first year of the school – of class sixth – there did take place yet another mishap, equally shattering. A lad from my village, also, from my class, whom I did not regard as worth my friendship, thinking that I was superior to him in terms of mental acumen, used to trouble me by asking me to give him my notebooks in which I did my homework or school-work. I obliged once or twice, not because I was a kind-hearted or benevolent fellow, but because I dreaded him: he was strong-bodied and haughty, too, alike *Shree Krishna.* Now that became his habit to ask for my Notebooks and I at times failed to complete my homework in time, due to setting of sun by the time he returned the Notebooks. In rural areas, it was a practice to go to bed immediately after sunset, for there was no electricity in villages those days; people made do with the kerosene lamps, that too, for short whiles only.

The boy at times also soiled my well-kept Note-books, which was intolerable for me. I kept my things – books, notebooks etc. – immaculately neat and clean, and also, without the ears dog-marked or folded. When it happened I started refusing to give him my notebooks, and to help him anymore. The matter of fact is that the boy was under the impression that since I was the topper of the class and a genius, if he emulated my work from my notebooks, he would be equally gifted. That however was not the case. Emulation through copying from notebooks cannot emulate the wisdom and giftedness of a brain. I was endowed with a brighter brain by God, that was my firm conviction.

He took up the issue with my mother as well, through his simpleton mother, but I reasoned with my kind as well as considerate mother, and she realised the dilemma I was in. She declined to oblige the chap astutely.

One evening, when it was getting dark, or it was the dusk, and it was the monsoon season, we heard the wailing voices rising from the house of the boy. We rushed thereto. The scene was utterly pathetic. We were told that the boy had consumed DDT.

'DDT? Why? Why should he have?', we expressed shock. We were apprehending in our childish beliefs that since the boy was short-tempered he might have tried to commit suicide.

Nevertheless, nobody wants to commit suicide, howsoever, irascible one might be. He had actually consumed DDT out of error. The error not of his, but of his parents. In the small hut-type *kutcha,* thatched house, they had put the bottle of DDT and the bottle of boy's medicines on the same terrace or niche. The boy as usual had gone to fields for grazing his cattle. When he returned, he was due to have his medicine and unintentionally, as was his wont, he poured the small bottle in his mouth. DDT it was! There was another bottle kept beside it, of course, containing the medicine. But it was late already; the malady had set in already.

The entire family got into utter panic as well as pandemonium. They rushed to the town, to the quack doctor, who had no wherewithal to deal with such calamities and emergencies. The boy is also reported to have been entreating to his father for saving him from the clutches of death. Death is such a ferocious phenomenon! He died as was destined. At that young age!

I should have felt sad; however, I did not. My trouble maker, my nagger, had died and I was relieved forever of his nagging behaviour, I thought instead. How childish was my thinking, now I realise! But it is too late now.

XXX



*19. Devil's Due*
*Enter Devil, the abuser cousin*

I was not good at anything, neither at studies, nor at anything else. I had been thrown out of a prestigious school living as we were at *Ajmer* with our parents, with my father serving in the Railways there as usual, as most of our family members were employed in the railways there, starting with the husband of *Kalaawatee Ammaa.* I being a spoilt brat alike my father who was a spoilt feudal product, was admitted to a prestigious school – St. Stephenson's School – but there they could not withstand my obscenities. Obscenities were in fact mingled with our blood as the feudal upbringing demanded that we were fed all sorts of vices, of which, abuses were the least offending stuff of all.

It so happened in due course of time that I and my elder sister both were admitted to this prestigious school, to which, only the children of high breed families – *zameendaars* and *taalukdaars* -- could be admitted. This concept of high breed was a unique concept concocted by the white rulers to subjugate gullible guys here. One day when my teacher – a young lady teacher – was trying to discipline me and teach me something, I went berserk as was my wont and I rebuffed her with the obscene remark, *"Behen kee ...... padhaatee tau kuchh hai naheen, maartee chillaatee rahtee hai...."* (meaning thereby, you ass of a female gender, instead of teaching us something sensible, you always keep on rebuking and scolding us….). This was a bombshell for the sober and serene 'sisters' of the prestigious school, unheard of ever in the serene as well as pious precincts of the school. They were scandalised no measure by this horrible remark of an innocent child. Immediately they called my father from his office and despite the sincere entreaties of the latter, the school administration thought it expedient to get rid of me, instead of taking any further risks of hearing any such tongue in their prestigious school.

And I was out; of course, not out of the stream of education; there were all sorts of educational outfits available there in that settlement of menial labourers. *Raamganj mauhallaa* in *Ajmer* was in fact the settlement of lower strata of society; and our parents and their other relatives were all living amidst them only despite their claims to the high breed upbringing at their native places. Maybe because they could not afford a better neighbourhood, or maybe their own living conditions in the rustic environs at the village were nothing better than those prevailing at *Raamganj*.

As the saying goes: 'like company, like character and demeanour!' I was a spoilt brat. Adept at every vice starting with drinking through smoking through eating meat and eggs, fucking lads, raping lasses, beating gentle boys of the *mauhallaa*, the neighbourhood *et al.* To add fuel to the fire, there were the sons of *Kalaawatee Ammaa* whose eldest son – *Raajoo Daadaa* – was an accomplished goon or bully of the area, a Don, as they would like to call him those days. The addiction to sexual activity is inexorable in fact; once it catches someone it never lets one go, however, desirous one might be to get rid of it. Libido is the most recalcitrant habit, it never leaves its addict. One must not fight against it advisably, otherwise one would get more and more depressed only. I was of this concept.

I was of the opinion that like all other tendencies, viz; hunger, thirst, nature's call, urination etc. which happen frequently as well as regularly, the desire to do or have sex also arises likewise and must be satisfied lest it should despoil the psyche of the person. And to substantiate my conviction I saw all around the society the youthful buxom lasses suffering for this reason; those who abstained from sexual activities did suffer from myriad diseases involving fits of epilepsy etc. And I noticed that those girls and lasses who did not try to check or control this desire, rather, fulfilled it by doing sex as and when warranted, did feel better psychologically and healthier physically. Also, I observed keenly that the girls who did sex looked prettier and more attractive and smooth-skinned in comparison to those who were abstemious and simpleton. Their demeanour was also amiable. The latter looked rough-skinned, unattractive and less pretty, and also, bad-tempered. Why Nature had dispensed like that I never could fathom that mystery, neither then, nor now in my long life. Maybe man's prescriptions to discipline or regulate the society are anti-Natural dispensation. Nature wants its creations to follow its rules or laws. Other than humans no other creature, even the plants and vines, the creepers, what to talk of other sub-human species, has any restriction or any inhibition about having or doing sex. Even the humans take no objection to their cattle having sex when the latter feel hot towards that; the cattle rather make a disturbing noise unless they get satiated sexually.

So that was my philosophy. Society and family norms prohibited having sex with close relatives, but the sexual desire does not obey any such injunctions or restrictions, it transcends every relational boundary. This is the only desire which unabashedly breaks every shield of relationship when aroused intensively. It's only after having exhausted its heat that one realises what one has done wrong, and that too against the social or familial norms as regards morality. And tries to hide it! Even those who come to know of those fouls in family fault-lines think it expedient to hide those fault-lines so as to avoid any further embarrassment as well as damage to the already fragile prestige of the family.

At our owned home, in fact, there were living the families of our father and of one of our uncles. Uncle too worked as a Station Master in the Railways there. My father had a large retinue of kids, even so, my uncle had a large retinue of kids. Myself being the eldest male issue, I had no qualms about having sex with the issues of my uncle, of course, those of fuckable or rape-able age. During those activities I had in fact come to realise that none of the partners with whom I had done sex objected to the obscene act as such, rather, after the first encounter when one did show at least some symbolic or sham hesitation, one would rather ask me of one's own volition to oblige him or her, for the sexual action is such an addictive habit.

But this sensation of libido or sexual desire when it rouses in the body, it seems like a perennial bliss throughout the body. And as soon as one finds a supportive partner and empties the bliss, the bliss goes away instantly. It feels like 'Paradise' having been 'Lost'. It reminded me of the well-known parable of the Bible wherein the

God forbade Adam and Eve in the garden of Eden to shun the apple of the garden, lest they should be thrown out of heaven. Indeed, as soon as one completes the sexual action, the entire bliss of heavenly experience subsides. Therefore, those who want to remain in perennial bliss ought to avoid doing sexual activity *per se* and, rather, must remain in bliss forever without doing sex. That is the import of the Biblical parable in my considered view.

But I enjoyed only instantaneous sex, notwithstanding the strong desire when it aroused within my body. Luckily or unluckily, there was no dearth of agreeable partners, as well, around me. And the secretive nooks in the sprawling house were not lacking; it could be done anywhere: inside the toilet, inside the bathroom, *et al,* particularly when the family elders could never suspect that their wards could break even the norms of chastity applicable within the family fold, that they could even indulge in incest. They were villagers, with rustic demeanours, and we were living in the city, where the norm was: 'everything goes!' And with the proliferation of romantic cinema, the sexual lust had become a predominant tendency in the urbanite environs.

Nonetheless, our uncle got transferred to *Sheekar,* or maybe he sought transfer to *Sheekar,* for there did develop some strains of rift in the two families. It is also quite possible that the elders eventually might have realised that their respective kids had been indulging in the forbidden incestual obscenities. Be that as it may, the long and short of the gory story is that they went away. One thing is for sure, that whosoever had been my sexual wife – male or female – homosexual or sexual – did not treat me honourably thereafter anymore. They treated me with disdain rather. The activity was profane no doubt when seen aloof from the actual scene of profane activity.

My sexual activities were nothing bizarre; in such a large family setup where two elders were having their young wives, it was usual that they would find some space – supposedly secluded one, but not really so secluded, given the children who had already come of age feigning to be sleeping around – for having sex. And it was umpteen number of times that I and even many of other siblings had noticed their parents doing sex openly, imagining in their false and sensuous notions that everybody must be asleep at the material juncture. There can be no other more titillating temptation than that of seeing someone doing sex to our side and, that too, openly, brazenly! That too, before a deserving youth!

Mother or father or uncle or aunt, those forbidding relationships don't matter in the scheme of Nature. Nature treats everybody as carnal body only, a sexpot only, a product of and for sexual activity.

I was growing up in such an environment, and without any pious or spiritual injunctions whatsoever.

With the departure of a large source of sexual satiety so readily available for me at home itself so far, I did feel a sudden sense of deprivation in my life. My own siblings I had tried only one or two and they were now flinching from the act feeling the moral hazards of the act, rather. They had developed a hatred towards me rather.

Just at that juncture, fortuitously, I got the news that one of our other uncles, who was supposedly an *ad hoc* teacher somewhere in the rural area but was *de facto* a beggar living on borrowings taken from the villagers, had shifted his homeless, shelter-less, hapless, family to our late grandmother's abandoned house at the village. I could guess easily that our aunt – the younger sister of my mother who was incidentally also the wife of this indolent uncle of mine – had at least two children who could be of use for my depravity as they had reached the age of puberty and could be abused easily, that is, for child-abuse. I thought that they would be perfectly innocent, unaware of this profane and obscene activity and would also not put up any resistance or make any hue and cry if handled deftly, that is, by simultaneously arousing their own sexual lust and fondling with their own young bodies. I had firm conviction that the body of a youth – both lad and lass – is a perfect reservoir of bliss. An entire volcano of lust can be aroused inside the youthful carnal body. Hot lava of lust can boil and erupt from every carnal body. With this firm belief in my mind, I ventured to the village. For Incest? Who bothers! That's not my problem! Child abuse? Bullshit! I want my satisfaction only. I don't care for the sentiments and tender feelings of those two teenagers at all!

For the family who were at our mercy, my arrival was like a celebration. Moreover, the lady was my mother's younger sister. She could not suspect in her wildest dreams that I was a devil, a paedophile, having arrived there to abuse her two young innocent children who did not even know the name of the obscene game, that I was going to defile both her children forever, and going to convert them into sex-pots whereafter they would ever indulge in self-sex if they did not get partners to satisfy their fire of sexual desire catalysed by me thus initially.

On the first evening, I demanded my aunt – *Mausee* – for cooking the dish of eggs and meat; they did not eat egg or meat though. She obliged by arranging somehow from somewhere. I did not bother that they lacked money and were poor people. I was not that sensitive. In my lust I was totally blind. Before my eyes I was seeing the young lad of eleven, who seemed to me like a lamb to a hungry wolf. Befittingly, or fatefully, on that day his father had made him to put on a very sexy and titillatingly glamorous coloured trousers; with that on, he seemed a perfect piece worth fucking immediately, on the spot, rather. The lad was in fact totally unaware of my nefarious intentions. He was thinking that I was his elder brother – cousin – quite advanced in age, of marriageable age indeed. Nonetheless, for me, every minute was passing like a month. That first day proved to me like an aeon until the night fell and I had taken my diet of meat and eggs, and also, some pills arousing sexual lust, of which, I was a connoisseur.

Becoming a perfect fire-ball of sex, I went to bed even as the sun had not set yet, to my aunt's surprise, and even to the surprise of all others. Otherwise, I was used to waking up till late in the night gossiping and chatting and bantering with simple village folks.

Then, I called the boy who was busy helping his mother, "*Eh, it's so cold, aren't you feeling cold?*"

"Yes, it's quite cold, *Bhaisaahab!*"

"What are you doing?"

"Helping my mother!"

"Don't do, come here; *mausee* will take care of everything!"

I also instructed *mausee* to let go of his son so that he could guard himself against the chilling cold outside. Who could imagine in one's wildest dreams that chilling cold was to begin in fact beneath the quilt of the youth and there would be no guard to protect the little unsuspecting boy within a few moments!

The boy came running and entered my quilt gleefully. I became so happy as if I had found a *rosogulla*, as if I had found a new young wife, as if it were my honeymoon night

I covered the boy from all sides immediately and fondled his soft body first of all. He was unsuspecting. I massaged his cheeks, his neck, his chest, his two fleshy as well as buttery breasts, his tummy, his legs, arms, all in the name of removing his cold. And the boy was happy, possibly somewhat aroused as well.

The sun had by now set. We both husband and wife – I and my sexpot - were beneath our quilt joined together, engrossed in the tussle, me to fuck and eat his flesh, he to somehow salvage his child's chastity. But the odds were widely dissimilar. I was a hefty twenty year old youth full of all sorts of vices of youth, he was merely an eleven year old adolescent, totally unprepared for this nefarious game, that too, by his own cousin whom he considered rather his saviour. The two souls, the man and the woman, whose son I was busy devouring and defiling nonchalantly as well as unhesitatingly, were totally unaware of the risks of making one's little kids sleep with the adolescents and youths on the same cot. They were awfully busy with their domestic chores as if nothing unusual was happening in the world around them at that momentous instant.

Here, I had my free time, ample time of a purposefully extended winter evening. I could continue with my sexual reverie for many hours if I liked, even in the eventuality of the fleshy body of the child having gone asleep.

During this period, quite a long time had elapsed, and both the man and his woman had also arrived. The room being very small, their cots were just touching ours. His mother was sleeping just next to him and father was sleeping just next to me. In other words, I was enjoying my sexual reverie just sandwiched between them. My

strokes were going on, the mouth of the boy was open and he was heaving. His mother was looking sympathetically at him just lying beside him. I suspect, she had realised what was underway beneath the quilt between us both. She could do nothing in such circumstances; otherwise too any sensible fellow could make out from the pose we were in: the boy was lying under my full body length. She, therefore, showed sympathy towards her son who was getting raped before her own eyes, just beside her. It could happen nowhere else on the earth! And none else could take such a risk than I did.

The foolish father, the indolent father, who could beget the babies but could not afford his own home, was bantering and chatting with me on topics like celibacy, *brahmcharya,* spirituality, morality *et al,* and I, while continuing with my depravity on the body of his adolescent son, was intermittently responding to his bantering by remarking like 'celibacy is divine' or 'morality is all in all', 'one must observe *brahmcharya,* that is really great', 'one should avoid doing dirty things or immoral things'. And the foolish man was praising me intermittently saying that my *sanskaars* were very good, and that I had not let my character get spoilt despite living in a city, and that it is what is called upbringing in a high breed family, a *khaandaanee* family.

As he was praising me, it was already late in the night. I had kept lying like that on the poor lad for about two hours, His mother would have certainly noticed all that sexual muck on the trousers of his son next day when she would have chosen to wash it. But what could a refugee do! Then I asked the boy to pull the trousers up and tie the knot, but he did not. He was in a state of deep moral shock. He kept lying like that as if his everything had been snatched away. I took pity upon him now in that state, and tied the knot of his *pyzaamaa* loosely. Still he kept on lying like that, as a dead fish, like a gang-raped lady; albeit I was singular, yet my action had the impact of more than the gangrape by a dozen youthful lads on a single lass. Had I taken another chance upon him he would not have objected anymore. It was all the same now. The field had been ploughed, the ground had been broken, the seed, any seed, could now be sown therein.

I think his carnal body enjoyed the rape but his mind which was framed by social norms did feel bad. He developed a dislike for me and also did no more treat me as his brother in his later life. He would have cursed me intensively, for which I suffered later on. That tale sometime later on, at an appropriate occasion.

XXX



## 20. Incest, The Price Of Refuge

*Enter mother*

We had settled at our new shelter, the refugee home, and it was almost six months now. My husband despite being employed temporarily at a far off school by grace of his relatives used to visit the village off and on, especially, on festive occasions. Whenever he happened to visit the village, his prime aim would be to take stock of the progress of his only son as regards the latter's education. He would test him in subjects of language, viz; *Hindee* and particularly, English. In English, he considered himself to be proficient, arguably. Arguably, for my nephew – the eldest son of my sister from *Ajmer* – was once heard commenting contemptuously, derisively rather, that my husband was nothing unusual as regards English teaching, for he had simply conned certain sentences of English and used to keep on repeating only those particular sentences. Moreover, he added, that my husband could not speak English, rather, he would insist on teaching Grammar to his pupils. That seemed to be true, too, for my husband always was heard asking the young chaps certain specific sentences of

*Hindee* of peculiar type, to be translated into English.

Anyway, there is no doubt that my husband was considered to be a gifted person as regards English tongue. Maybe, for there was none else in the entire area to test the veracity of this fact. Moreover, prior to that, his father and elder brother were also considered as equally deft at English tongue.

My husband's *Hindee* knowledge was equally good; and he had some little knowledge of *Urdoo*, too. He was satisfied with the progress and performance of his reportedly prodigious son at school. Nonetheless, once when he visited the village, he asked my son to read a *Hindee* poem from his text book; it was regarding the valour of the legendary queen of *Jhaansee*, a famous historic figure. When he enquired about the prosaic version of the poem, whatever my son explained, my husband was not satisfied with that. To this, I explained that whatever his teachers at school had taught him he was reproducing only that. How could he know beyond the ignorance of his teachers? My husband was not satisfied nonetheless, and lamented the lack of knowledge and inferiority of the teachers at the school of his son.

My son commented, "Is it that even *Hindee* they do not know well? I thought, only English was the tongue that was meant to be learnt and taught!"

I and my husband chuckled. My husband responded to his son's lament, "*Hindee* is a very tough language in fact!"

It was the winter season, possibly the month of December, with a weather of chilled cold those days. My nephew – the eldest son of my sister, in whose homestead we were sheltered as destitutes – happened to visit us that winter. This guy actually had no job; he was neither studying anywhere. He was living the life of a vagabond. His habits were, too, not praiseworthy. I knew, he was having so many vices the lads living in urbanite environs get afflicted with. Smoking, meat-eating, indulging in sexual activities, flirting with young lasses, fucking young lads, depravity, *et al*. Those were considered as virtues in urbanite environs inculcated as those had been from the tinsel world – the cinema, whereas the same traits were considered as vices in rustic environs. The cinema in those days was breaking many taboos. To the better or worse, nobody could vouchsafe.

This sister of mine was having a contingent of eight issues, a number exceptionally hilarious by even the standards of those days. In fact, my sister and brother-in-law were not able to beget issues for years together after solemnisation of their marriage; whereas in those backward societies, the marriage and then begetting maximum number of children was the sign of greatness as regards womanhood and manhood. Food one might forsake but not the wedding, woman and wooing. So when for four or five years after their marriage, my sister and her husband did not choose to produce any feline of issues, the village folks, especially, elder ladies got alarmed: 'Was the woman barren, sterile?'

She was not, nor was the man – my brother-in-law. Getting stung by this scathing criticism and derisive contempt, they started producing living beings with a vengeance. Had there been no restraint of nine months on the timeline for begetting human babies, they would have produced one baby a day. They were in such a rage! So they produced eight, a few causalities in between, too. Eight surviving kids!

This nephew at the loose end was a brat sort of lad. He often visited the village and bragged amongst the village folks who were but gullible guys, simple hearted by that time. The exodus of Britishers was hardly twenty years past yet, and the sense of innocence as an offshoot of wretchedness had not left the psyche of the populace at large.

But this nephew of mine was not an innocent or gentle guy, I knew it well, as was betrayed by his misdemeanours off and on.

My husband was also in the village incidentally at that time; those were possibly the holidays of Christmas or New Year, I am not sure. For we were living in their house, we were obliged to welcome the issues of our sister with pleasing countenances as well as whole heartedly; otherwise, too, there was no reason why we should not have; they were after all young children! We were their close relatives, too!

That evening – the evening I am referring to - my husband had returned from the town. As already mentioned in so many words, my husband had a large following at the town. He had brought or bought a cloth for *pyzaamaa* for my son. The texture and colour of the cloth was extremely glamorous and seductive by all measures. My son was initially reluctant to put on that *pyzaamaa,* for that aroused the sexual feeling in the body and legs; not only of the wearer, but also, of others towards the wearer. Human body is such a magnetic contrivance! It attracts the other bodies towards itself. And seductive and glamorous clothes add to that vice immensely. Paedophiles may be activated at slightest spur of this sort.

However, my husband being a buffoon did not have such sensibilities. For him, the world and society were a deaf and dumb entity, and *sans* any feelings, just like himself. His knowledge of social sentimentalities was very shallow. He insisted that my son put on the gaudy *pyzaamaa* for it had been donated by someone free of cost at the time, and also, stitched almost for naught. Despite his reluctance, my son put it on; assured in his convictions that there would be no risk of abuse – child abuse – at least in the home. At school, of course, it might arouse sensual feelings in the hearts of girls in the class -- whom he did not choose to love despite the instigations of the former – or maybe in the minds of paedophile adults.

It was cold, as I told. My nephew being an urban brat loved eating eggs and meat. In our house, we were vegetarians. Strict ones. But my nephew insisted that eggs be bought and meat be cooked for him. I did not know how to cook eggs or how to cook meat; so my nephew took it upon himself to arrange everything. My husband was not around at the material time. It was arranged in such a way that it did not come to the notice of my husband. It was not a tough task, not a big deal, for my husband was a duffer and could be fooled quite easily. Even if he had noticed the meat being cooked, it might be pretended that coloured spices had been added to the dishes, that's why it was red or so, and he would have been made to believe that lie possibly.

A youthful lad of twenty, my nephew had his fill of meat and eggs and spices, well before it all could come to the notice of that another brat as well as buffoon of my husband. I hastened to wash the utensils and everything was well settled.

After my husband and all the rest had had food, we were set to go to bed. In villages those days, the time to go to bed was immediately after sunset; there were no electric lights etc. Merely a slender wick of the earthen or wooden lamp would come to the rescue of villagers, that too, for an hour or so. For the kerosene that was used in the lamp cost dearly by the standards of villagers, us included all the more, given our wretched financial condition.

I had not yet finished the kitchen chores. My nephew took to the bed: the middle bed in the small-sized room wherein there was no space left in between the cots after adjusting all the three cots. In fact, many people were to be accommodated for sleeping in the small-sized room: me, my husband, our twenty year old nephew, my eleven year old son, my six year old daughter, another baby girl of over one year. For those were the days of chilled cold, it was cozy rather to sleep sandwiched between the cots and beds. Yet such circumstances have their pitfalls. The phony contrivances like relationships do not work when the cobras of anatomical deformities and arousals raise their hoods. My nephew had gone to his designated bed on purpose immediately after having a sumptuous food of meat and eggs.

After some time, he hailed my son as well. My son was innocent; he could not suspect any ill-will, or any harm at least from a lad who was related to my son as his elder cousin, whom he called *'Bhaisaahab!'* (elder brother). I had assigned my son some petty domestic tasks which he was performing, but the elder lad persisted in his bleats hailing my son. I should have been alarmed. But I did not have any *sanskaars* to that effect in my psyche; how could I arouse the *vigyaan* of suspicion about what was intended by my nephew or what was going to happen!

My nephew asked me that I ought to take care of the remaining household chores, and that he and my son were going to sleep. He offered the excuse that it was very cold outside, and it was expedient to go to bed early. They aver that suspicion is a bad trait, but I hold

that suspicion is a very effective means to avert damages or dents that may be inflicted on life in the absence of this instinct of suspecting everybody invariably.

My son went gleefully, unaware of what was going to happen to his virgin body. He was totally innocent about such things. He was a village boy, never having come across such depravity of urban brats. Moreover, now he was sheltered in the cave of wolves, his parents being homeless! Where could he escape! How could he raise an alarm!

The young lad soon started off with his depraved activity. He was fully aroused having had his fill of seductive and intoxicating food.

As my son disclosed to me later, the elder lad took the small, tender hand of my kid in his hand under the quilt. The boy thought that his elder 'brother' was simply playing something. He was after all his elder *'bhaisaahab'*! How could he suspect such an obscene act on the former's part, that too, in one's own house, beside one's parents who were sleeping just close by, whose breaths could be felt on one's face. For the cots were laid close by without a gap in between. My son was of the type who always kept on harping on the refrain that he would ever remain a celibate, a *Brahmachaaree.*

In the meantime, I had finished my chores and come to sleep beside them. My husband was also back from outside and he was on his cot on the opposite side of the middle bed on which the lad was fucking my kid in our very presence and proximity.

On the other hand the small kid was showing grimaces on his face, for his piety, chastity and virginity were being snatched away forever by none other than his elder cousin. Moreover, he was being afflicted with a *sanskaar,* of which, he would never ever get rid thereafter. Sexual *sanskaar* once created is such a strong *sanskaar,* that craves its repetition again and again, and never gets satiated, rather aggravates day by day.

The activities under the quilt were quite conspicuous by their tumult, however, I was clueless as to what to do in such crucial and critical circumstances of obscene proportions and having moral hazards. It was a matter of prestige. If the matter came to light, there was the question of how to handle its aftermath. My husband was there on the opposite side of the scene, whereas the depravity was being enacted literally under our noses. Our kid was being fucked just next to our bodies, and we could do nothing!

I was watching my son in that depraved condition helplessly as well as cluelessly. I could find no way out of that situation. My son was paying the price of our seeking refuge in their house. He alone was paying the price of refuge by getting abused. In the presence of us both – the indolent husband and his clueless wife. It continued for quite a while. The depraved person relished it fully, and for too long, and we could do nothing.

Ultimately, Nature only came to the rescue of my kid; *pyzaamaa* of my son was soiled, and it did not dry till next morning. Not to speak of the blood and semen stains quite obvious on the *pyzaamaa* which I could see quite apparently the next day when I took it for washing. I knew quite well what had happened. The boy was feeling excruciating pain between his legs for days together.

My son's countenance got totally withered thereafter, not only the next day, but ever thereafter. His *pyzaamaa* was having stains of profuse bleeding as well. Neither I could ask what the matter was, nor he could tell me. But he left no stone unturned to make his face as grievous as he could thereafter. And now it was unto us to realise what had happened. Our little innocent son had paid the first instalment of the lease rent for our wretched and depraved shelter. We – man and woman -- were, however, unscathed so far; nonetheless, not sure for how long!

XXX



## 21. Not Spared Even My Sister Of Six

*Enter Mother*

Next day when the night fell, my son refused to sleep with his cousin – my nephew. He had been morose throughout the day as if everything he had for this birth had been snatched away from him: his chastity. Of which, he was so fond. In his fancies and convictions he abhorred those wretched people who fell prey to depravity and such sexual abuses under the circumstances. For the first time he now realised that it had nothing to do with one's character or valour, rather, it all depended on the circumstances, or the fate, as they call it, for simplicity's sake.

My son had gone to the school in that stained *pyzaamaa* only the next day; what else could he do? He could not disclose his shame! Nor was there the practice of putting on a freshly cleaned dress everyday for going to school. Whatever impression his classmates and, more so, his girl admirers might have made seeing his *pyzaamaa,* nothing could be helped.

When my son expressed his reluctance to sleep with his *'bhaaisaahab'* the next night, my suspicion that the elder lad had fucked my kid was confirmed. Still, nothing could be done. Circumstances were such that nothing could be done. We could not throw the lad out; we were sheltered in their homestead only, rather. They could throw us out instead! To allege that their son had done child abuse with our kid was like inviting an obscene trouble which nobody would subscribe to despite realising in one's heart that the allegation labelled was correct. In such sexual matters, especially, of child-abuse or incest, everybody chooses to hush up the matter; for that is the easiest way; for the remedy in such cases is far graver than the disease itself.

On his refusal, I agreed, and he slept with me with my little daughter and me on the already very small cot. His father insisted on my kid sleeping with the latter's *'bhaisaahab'*, but the kid did not gather courage to subject himself to another round of sexual exploitation at the hands of a grown up relative who was rather supposed to protect him from such sexual abuses. How pathetic it was! How grave was the crime of my husband; it was not merely the indolence and incapacity to earn his living – the provision of *rotee, kapdaa* and *makaan* – but my husband's actions were resulting in such sexual exploitation of his issues at the hands of our sham benefactors. This nasty truth my deranged husband could never fathom. He was such a mad-skull! Such a madcap!

I asked my six year old daughter to sleep rather with the lad; and the innocent kid gladly agreed, for she was unaware of the obscenity as well as depravity awaiting her ahead. My son was relieved that night, but constantly in psychological scare of the elder lad thereafter in his life, I felt palpably.

And the next day, my daughter's countenance was morose and darkened. And she expressed reluctance to sleep with the lad the next night. I was doubly sure now that the paedophile depraved lad had abused my six year old child – the daughter – too. Shamelessly! Unbeknown to my duffer husband! However, all apparent to me.

When none of the two kids was willing to sleep with the depraved lad, the abusive lad, a moral crisis was engendered in the house. The house was too small to accommodate everybody. The space was limited whereas my husband was having unlimited capacity to produce issues, unconcerned about where to accommodate them, or how to feed them, not to speak of how to save them from being fucked or raped by the close relatives or so-called sham benefactors themselves. My husband could not even imagine that such a depraved thing could happen. However, that was

happening despite his innocence as well as ignorance. That's why the wise ones have said: ignorance is bliss. And that is the reality of the world, the depravity, the incest, the child abuse *et al.* The world is not as moral and as innocuous as we think it is!

Despite our cajoling, my son did not agree for further fucking by his *'bhaisaahab'*; he went to the extent of revolting even. His *'bhaisaahab'* tried to assure him that nothing would happen in a mock assurance, but to no avail. The resentment of my son aroused suspicion now in the mind of my husband, too. Slow to understand everything as he was!

I made my daughter only to sleep with the depraved lad, for that was less dangerous proposition in my view. The lad could not enjoy as much fucking a six year old girl as he could relish fucking an eleven year old sex-pot of a cherub lad, I mused. I was sad nonetheless.

The next day, when my son had gone to school, my husband raised the issue with me. The issue of sexual abuse of his issues by the nephew. I expressed mock ignorance, for that was the only recourse supposed of me in those dire circumstances. Our fates were hanging by thin wires. We could not take umbrage against our sham benefactors, nor could we complain to them against their beloved eldest son, though a brat. Rather, we ourselves might lose the precariously availed shelter in the process.

In the absence of my husband, I accosted the depraved boy who was there only for enjoying depravity and to practise child-abuse on the bodies of my innocent issues. Naturally, he expressed innocence and refuted the charge. I knew he was lying. I warned him that his uncle had come to know of what he had done, and that he had better run away the next day from the village. And he fled from the scene, after abusing my only son of eleven and the elder daughter of six.

Returning from school my son enquired where his *'bhaaisaahab'* was and when I disclosed that he had gone to his city, he felt obviously relieved. Still he enquired, "Why? He was to stay here long as he was telling."

"But your father got angry with him."

"Why?"

"Because he cooked eggs and meat in the house and using the utensils of the house, and that the utensils had become thus unusable for the house, for the vegetarians." I replied and added further that the utensils had been washed by me well after cooking the meat and that now there was no sign left of the meat or egg in the utensils and we could use them. How reasonable I

was in saying this I did not know but that was the only logical argument I could offer in those embarrassing environs or circumstances. Also, we had no other utensils in the house which we could use! My soul was crying. My son and my daughter had both been child-abused by none other than our close relative only, and our helplessness was such that we could do nothing, for we were simply wretched refugees, dependent on the rapist for the shelter!

Thereafter, I observed as if the bottom of the pots had been cracked or broken. Both my kids were seen masturbating in the bed or rubbing their sexual organs off and on whenever they found the isolation and solitude. I tried to dissuade them by beating them and insulting them, but sexual deformities cannot be helped by such punishments; insults and beatings have no effect at all, for what can be more insulting than the child abuse for a kid, and also, what can be more painful for a child than the child-abuse! When the desire for sexual activity gets aroused no power in the world, rather, no phenomenon of relationships in the world, can stop it from getting satiated. And sex once done is done forever. It is the sweetest experience of the whole Creation which once relished can never be forsaken.

However, I being a female, and that too, in a feudal and depraved set-up of indolent and inactive males, could do nothing. I had no wherewithal to guard against such obscene activities. Depravity was the hall-mark of feudal societies, however, done clandestinely.

XXX



22. Sickness And Vaidyajee At Town

*Enter protagonist*

After the incident of child-abuse by our close relative in our own house, rather, in the house of our benefactors, my psyche was shattered irreparably, inexorably. I had as though drowned myself in a sea of depression and disgrace in my own eyes; I had as though been defiled forever; I was no more pure and chaste. My body had been made impure, I thought. I generated extreme amount of angst and hatred towards that adult of mine then, and throughout my life thereafter I kept on cursing him whole-heartedly. I had no respect for him anymore, although outwardly I did the formality of being normal. The reason was that my sexual behaviour had been changed for the worst thereafter. Whenever I recalled that horrendous episode, my body got sexually charged and arousal took place instantly and then there was no

way I could help it, except letting it through. Self-sex became my norm. I did not have courage to indulge in other sex, for that much courage I did not have. That was my mistake. I had developed the notion, however, that flirting with females, the girls, was a bad thing, whereas now I realise that there is nothing as 'bad' as regards doing sexual activity with females or beautiful girls. After all their anatomy and body is meant for that purpose only. If not me, someone else would use that body. And experience showed that others were enjoying sexual activity with lovely girls and were much happier than I was with my abstinence and self-sexual activities. I have never remained the same innocent and enthusiastic chap thereafter. That episode of my rape at the hands of an elder relative haunts me constantly.

I even cursed the depraved criminal by asking the God almighty that He might give the criminal a daughter who would be a beautiful yet deranged one. By that time, of course, the lad had not been married formally, though he was not a celibate. Still I fancied like that in my rage. I intended to avenge myself upon him and his family. At the time of my abuse, he was not even married.

Later, decades later, I found out to my pleasant surprise and relief of heart that he had got a very pretty daughter, but she was deranged by birth. I felt so relieved yet somehow shocked. I thanked God, the *Dharma*, thinking that '*dhamma* had worked!' Even as, my wounds had been avenged.

The child abuse had aggravated my habit of self-sex and it had become a source of extreme bliss for me. Whenever I intended bliss at cheapest cost, I resorted to that, even as, that was easily available. God has dispensed like that only for me!

But the psychological trauma had disrupted my body and mind. I fell sick after some time. My father as I told did not stay with us; he had gone to his *ad hoc* job as a sham teacher.

When I fell sick I felt I had been impregnated by the boy, for I did not have the idea that a male could not get impregnated. Still I got scared what if I became pregnant. Maybe that is why I fell sick.

In the absence of my father, my mother called *Modhoo chaachaajee* for help, for taking me to *vaidyajee* at the town. *Modhoo chaachaajee* brought a bullock cart to take me to the town, for in the village, we had no other wherewithal to take the patients to the *vaidyajee*. There was no one in the village who could take care of the petty diseases of the villagers. In our family, rather, there was the notion that illness was the result of

sin: the sin of not following the rules of health, the rules of Nature. My grandfather normally was heard quoting from *Gaandhee* that falling sick was a sin. And my father was one step further ahead of his father: he even got angry, instead of showing sympathy with the patient, the sufferer. The reason was that he did not have money and taking any treatment entailed expenditure, therefore, the better way was to propagate the philosophy that falling sick was the result of sin.

Nonetheless, in my case, it was sin literally that had made me sick. The psychological trauma had disrupted the rhythm of my body and I had fallen sick.

*Modhoo chaachaajee* took yet another uncle along with him in the bullock cart. When I was being carried in the cart, those were the days of spring season, neither cold, nor hot, still I was covered under a quilt in the bullock cart. Both the elders kept on chatting throughout the way. My psyche had become so afflicted with the sexual mishap that I apprehended that those two adults could both abuse me in the cart alike my '*bhaaisaahab*' did, and I could do nothing in that eventuality. Throughout the way I kept on praying to God to save me from the clutches of relatives who could exploit my body for sexual abuse. However, the two adults were not amused to relish my body, especially, of a sick body. And I thanked God. I had lost faith in the chastity of elders and relatives whosoever.

Moreover, I was aggrieved for that obscenity had deformed the system of my sex incorrigibly, and I had become a sex addict, on which, I had no control. That was a great harm done to my physical body, apart from engaging my mind forever. I became a totally deformed person sexually. Full of hatred and suspicion towards all the elders.

*Vaidyajee* looked like the olden day *rishis* (sages). He treated the patients with *Aayurvaidic* medicines and charged almost naught. He prescribed pulses of *Moong* and *chapaatee* as the diet during disease.

Having returned safely, that is, without having been abused sexually by another set of adults, I felt relieved and thanked God.

My mother was, however, very caring. She caressed me so well that I got cured soon. And started living though a changed person in entirety! I was never the same child thereafter!

XXX



*23. Autobiography vs Fiction*
*Enter protagonist*

I don't know why I am dubbing this autobiography as a novel! This seems to be the symptom of my split personality, due to which, in real life, after a certain point in time, the passenger of the journey of this carnal body did start harbouring the notion that he was lost somewhere. And this notion persisted ceaselessly. Delusion only it was after all! Otherwise, had I been lost during the life's journey through carnal body, could I ever be able to present this intriguing account? Well, I am cloaking this autobiography under the fanciful sheet of a novel as if to self-deceive myself. My tale is in fact the tragic tale of a personality's crash – of a split personality.

So far I have not been able to decide the central character – the protagonist - of this story; he might have died somewhere -- in grade six – getting hurt by the sarcastic tones of his teacher. He has no cognizable existence! No existence, maybe! The mathematics teacher having written a problem of maths – quite a simple one, of course – on the blackboard, and whipping the tender stick on his palms with a shuddering sound in a flaunting fashion, whatever he had commented addressing him – the protagonist – does still resonate and echo in my ears incessantly:

"Well, you, do tell me, you, the *Mahaarathee!*"

*Hm hm hm hm....* The entire class burst into a loud laughter.

Didn't laugh if anyone, it was the one, only he – the

*Mahaarathee!* Engrossed unto oneself, somewhat piqued and irritated at oneself, or possibly alike what, or possibly somewhat humiliated!

*"Aachaaryajee!* We don't get the facility and opportunity to study at home!", he had averred in a piteous tone; followed by a loud laughter once again from the class, the innocent kids, but somewhat queer, somewhat crazy. The mathematics teacher after immediately whipping the twig-stick on his tender and small palms remorselessly and dispassionately had rejoindered, "Scoundrel! How smart in offering excuses! Do all others get facilities and proper opportunities at home?"

*"Hm hm hm hm....."*

All were agape looking towards my face; it was only me this time, who was laughing with an open heart – all alone – most likely alike a crazy soul, gone mad, as was apparent from the peering eyes of the teacher which were fixed on my face, looking towards me, speechless, dumbfounded and befuddled. At my temerity! Of unbridled laughter! In the class! Before the teacher!

XXX



21. Sawaa Rupayaa *And Feudal Conceit*
*Enter protagonist*

Presently, if I venture to take you in front of my father introducing him as the villain of my autobiography, the novel, pray don't get startled or befuddled; and in your confusion or desperation, pray don't hasten to christen me the villain of the story instead, and my father as the protagonist or hero. This is a novel, and you would enjoy it by accepting my convictions as such which are going to be truisms in due course.

Now see, this is the winter season – the biting chilled cold of January 1970 – and I am obliged to stand beside the grandest old lady of the combined family of this feudal set up, with an aim, of course, with some purpose. The grandest old lady – she was the grandmother of my father and the aunt of my grandfather – was sitting there in the sunshine deriving whatever little energy she could from the sunbeams in that chilling cold outside, on that upraised highland of feudal lords. It need not be told that she was sitting on a straw or rope cot beside a potted big plant of *Tulsee,* the Basil.

My baby heart however feels hesitant to beg a pittance even from the grandest mother of the family, musing that the whole lot of responsibility for taking care of my necessities of existence should fall upon my begetters, my parents, who had enjoyed the sexual intercourse in exchange for my arrival on this planet. How can, then, they send me with begging bowl to someone forsaking their moral responsibility totally and shamelessly? My parents only are in fact responsible for having begotten me in this existential universe as an outcome of their dissipation as well as libido. It is they only who need to fulfil all my requirements of existence as a recompense for their sensual sins; my life-wave requires an infinite expanse and infinite medium for uninhibited progression and propagation. Alike the ripples generated in a water pond that get created as an outcome of throwing a stone therein if only callously, and which start spreading outwards automatically towards the infinite shore! I wish at the moment in my state of utter anguish that there were no shores for the propagation of the life-waves; that there should be no outer limit to the expansion of life's waves!

But on the contrary, I am finding that one of the two passengers of carnal bodies who have begotten me impertinently and callously due to their dissipation and depravity, does not bother at all about such tender and unblemished feelings and higher aspirations being nourished in my child's mind. That species called 'father' is reportedly to be employed somewhere else: 'He is in teaching job at a far off land!', is the explanation given by my kindly mother. He only is responsible for my straitjacket financial condition and of hers, too!

'Teacher he is! Well, have all the people of this area been educated then? That he has gone abroad for teaching the people at other places! Is there no need for any teaching or teaching staff in this area so that my father has had to go far off – about 100 kms away from home, the village – for imparting education, or for selling the instructions?', I muse.

However, No; a teacher is least bothered about such concerns, about the literacy or illiteracy of a geographical area, or of even any individual; he is basically a person indulged in marketing – a salesman – a salesman of education, the instructions!

It's only yesterday that my class-teacher - that is, the teacher assigned with the task of collecting fees from a particular class - had summoned me to his seat, and had shouted in a rebuking as well as condemning tone, "Why, *Arvind!* Why don't you deposit the fees? How many times it takes that you have to be reminded for depositing your fees! It seems your 'memory' is pretty weak and freak!"

The rest of the class was silent – they didn't laugh – yet I felt as if I had been stripped to my skin and felt extreme shame and humiliation. The same classmates and playmates who are all praise for my brain-power – which includes the 'memory' too – when they would hear such paradoxical sermons – the Gospel precepts, the *Ved-Vaakya* -- from my class teacher in front of every Tom, Dick and Harry of the class, what impression would they derive about me; they would certainly start doubting their wisdom. The same teacher, who is incidentally our *Sanskrit* teacher as well, has he not eulogised me in front of the class umpteen number of times? Has he not quoted me as an exemplar of intelligence for the pupils of the class, both male and female?

Nonetheless, in the name of fees – the tuition fees – which is nothing but paltry sum of only a few *paise*, only 125 or 131 paise in all, that is, one and a quarter of a rupee – the same teacher strips me naked, humiliates me – a child – before the entire class full of duffers, with little concern for his own convictions and proclamations about my giftedness, without any concern about my tender feelings: uttering senselessly, 'Your memory seems to be quite weak and freak!' I for myself consider myself a totally unfit subject or culprit for this reprimand, this punishment, this humiliation. I find myself unable to fathom where I am at fault, how I am careless, personally me, the child, the student?

Still, what the mother could do, too? For last six months too it's only she who has been arranging to pay the fees, out of the pittance somehow collected in her small wallet; not from the money received from my father, even as, she never got a *paisaa* from her husband; rather, her husband on the contrary snatched away money from her, whatever she tried to save. She paid me out of the bounty she created out of money received from her parents, from her caressing as well as affectionate mother. To call it a bounty would be an exaggeration even, probably. However, even father, whenever he came to visit here from his place of posting, he managed to snatch away even that paltry sum from my mother by deceit, conceit, or through use of devilish force. At times, the matter reached a stage where he did not flinch from even using his carnal force against my tender mother's body. Only recently, when he had come on the occasion of *'Badaa Din'* – the Christmas holidays, he had flogged the back of the mother by sticks many a time. Mother had got fainted several times in the process even. A broken stick is still seen there lying in the courtyard as if testifying to the bestial cruelty of my father – of course, in use, of late, for shooing away the dogs and bitches from the house – a stick broken in the process of flogging the back of my mother at the hands of a virile and virulent father! A villain! As if a testimony, a witness! Ever reminding about his devilish nature!

This was possibly the cause behind my mother not being able to pay my fees this time.

I catch hold of my mother immediately on waking up this morning: "Mother, my fees, please!"

"What to do?" I could hear very vividly this unspoken exclamation or sigh of desperation emanating from her throat, coupled with exhalation, and reflected in her crimson eyes. I relented helplessly, seeing my mother's predicament thus.

Nonetheless, after dispensing with certain daily chores I once again caught up with my hapless mother, for I didn't have any other option. I shrieked and said, "My fees! *Sawaa Rupayaa!* One and a quarter rupee! I get humiliated at school! For no fault of mine! Because of the indolence of you people! My mates would consider me a wretch!"

And nobody wants to be considered a wretch, even a wretch does not want to be considered as such. I utter all this coming as this did from the deep crevices of darkness and gloom in my child's heart and bosom. My mother nevertheless kept mum still.

"You people can't afford even to pay a fees of paltry sum of *Sawaa Rupayaa*? A rupee and a quarter? Wretches are you all! Wretches! Wretches you all!"

This time the mother did writhe in agony. Sharing her mental agony due to this humiliation with her indolent husband, she called her husband names several times and abused him *in absentia*; then she asked me, "Wretches no doubt these people are! No doubt! And they call themselves high breed and of high pedigree! High *khaandaanee!* Ironically, they are considered a high pedigree in the entire area! They pride themselves and arrogate against others! *Badvaale!* Come ask me, whoever wants to know the internal story and reality of these people!"

"Even a rupee and a quarter, *Sawaa Rupayaa,* you do not possess, mother?", I happen to ask her with extreme curiosity as if I could not believe my mother, that there could be a family with several kids and babies in the household, which didn't have even a rupee and a quarter. Whereas they had already taken a plunge into the cesspool of begetting half a dozen issues! Whereas they had taken an adventure of such huge proportions as begetting half a dozen issues!

Is there no punishment prescribed for producing babies? Is there no sentence to be given by the legal courts for this heinous crime perpetrated against innocent creatures – the babies? Are there no financial norms set for producing children in the society? Every Tom, Dick and Harry has been practising one's expertise on producing children, getting absolutely blind towards those norms? When they have taken cudgels to beget issues, they should at least have the guts to earn and have at least this much money: a rupee and a quarter, *Sawaa Rupayaa*! Why my mother was side tracking the crucial issue, I could not fathom?

However, this time it was the turn of my mother who wailed and wailed piteously. Somehow checking the surge of tears in her eyes, taking me in her lap and putting certain kisses on my chubby and cherub cheeks, she did exclaim, "My dear! Piece of my heart! When there is absolute dearth, it is of little consequence whether it's one and a quarter of a rupee or it is a single *paisa*; all is the same! Do you think, money is more precious and dear to me than you are? I value the price of these entreaties of yours  for your paltry fees in lacs of rupees each! I shall never ever find myself disentangled from the psychic pangs of your psychic pain and anguish; I shall never ever be able to offload the weight of your words from my heart!......"

Mother was gibbering incoherently and unintelligibly I could not know what or what not.

Nevertheless, I was thrilled to be in her lap and poking in her lovely face which was still full of youthfulness. How enchanting were those two eyes of hers – how everything in her anatomy – in the body of my mother – was attractive! Why needed I give her pain? Possibly, I might solve the riddle or the questionnaire of life myself, too!

"Mother, shall I go beg of the grandest mother?"

"But how many times should she oblige us by giving? How many times has she given us!"

"But she is the mother of all – all and sundry – in this vast family circle. She ought to give everybody every time! Why should one suffer deprivations until she is capable of giving something from her resources? I, however, did harbour the notion at that age that the grandest mother had an inexhaustible treasure trove of the entity so trivial and worthless as money.

And with the first rays of the rising sun as though riding them, I had approached the grandest mother, rushing blindly from my home to hers. The Sun god was there just in front of me riding its chariot yoked on to seven horses.

To my misfortune or hard luck, certain members of the large family tree of the *Daadee* too had congregated around her with the intention of warding off the chill of the winter season. Now, how could I have begged for a rupee and a quarter – *Sawaa Rupayaa* - under such straitjacket circumstances? Alms? Alms for a paltry sum of as little as a rupee and a quarter merely?

XXX



## 25. Shaitaano Bhav!

*Enter protagonist*

*'Aachaarya Devo Bhav! Maatri Devo Bhav! Pitri Devo Bhav!'* The *Sanskrit* teacher whom I call as the 'Salesman of *Sanskrit*' – of course, clandestinely, in my heart and mind – after commanding the pupils to con and memorise by heart these three proverbs of the lesson – the three all-pervasive, universal as well as conventional lines, himself is enjoying sitting in the sunshine outside: with legs rested on the table, pointing the toes towards the Sun god, possibly on the pretext of finalising the accounts of the tuition fees, as I am surmising in my mind sitting idly.

*"Arvind! Eh Arvind!"*

My eyes turned towards the source of voice; and found that *'Mahaarathee'* – what's his real name I don't know, but the other day when the teacher had called him callously and insensitively by the appellation of derisive term *'Mahaarathee'*, he has since become for me a *'Mahaarathee'* only for all practical purposes, so much so that his real name – the name given by his parents – has drowned in the dense darkness of oblivion along with whole of its memorial energy and potential; he was hailing me: *"Arvind! Eh Arvind!* What's the meaning of these lines?"

All at once I got catapulted into the memory lane, even as, the recent incidents and misdemeanour of the teacher on the day gone by resurfaced on the canvas of my mind. Whatever did take place today in the morning at my home, i.e. when I was standing before my grandest grandee in the chilling cold – for quite a while – suffering humiliation and jeers of her grandchildren, it was only because of this teacher, due to his mendacity and lack of sensitivity. *Daadee* – the affectionate and aged grandma – for a while – had thought that I had gone in her vicinity without any specific purpose, merely to enjoy morning sunbeams, or to seek company of the grandma due to my affection and reverence towards her. Nevertheless, the time to go to school was approaching fast: the same school, the *Vidyaa-Mandir* (the temple of skills) – which is nothing short of a shop of skills, and if one does not have wherewithal to pay fees, if one does not have capacity to arrange uniform of the school, one cannot be admitted to seek skills and education in that shop, irrespective of the fact that one is very brilliant, one is exceptionally gifted one, and also, eligible one to seek admission – the time to go to the same shop for buying the right to get skills and education after paying the fees, was approaching fast.

The assistant of time called a watch or a clock was found nowhere in the countryside, in no household, not to speak of the household of my wretched parents. Majority of the folks determined and ascertained the status of time by watching the pattern and position of shade of the sun during the day, and the position of stars and constellations during the night. And cock was the Nature's alarm-clock for heralding the onset of dawn every day!

My shadow getting dwindled was about to touch the deadline. I was getting impatient. If I did not beg for *Sawaa Rupayaa* - rupee one and a quarter – that would be alike the death, implying a great humiliation at school during the day: that *shaitaanic* incarnation, the fees collector, that is, my class teacher, would strike off my name from the register as well as the class. If I beg for a rupee and a quarter, that's in turn such a contemptible act – begging for such a trifling thing as fees! 'Begging is a contemptible act!' This has all along been taught to us. That the beggars ought to be looked down upon has been the intonation given to us all along since

our childhood by our elders in family and outside in the society. Such a complex conundrum and an inexperienced tender undeveloped mind! What is the basis for deciding right and wrong? The skill, the idea for pondering over such intractable issues had not developed yet; whatever had been taught as right was right only, notwithstanding the fact that the conscience revolted against its veracity, did refuse to accept its validity. I got utterly perturbed.

I, feeling uncomfortable in this situation or recalling to mind the imminent humiliation at school in the class where there were so many devils – well, the *shaitaan* does dwell in the hell only – did conceive a stratagem in my mind to somehow reach the ear of the grandee and succeed in that; and without forewarning her, without hinting anything to her, catching her ears and covering them on both sides by my small palms, whispered in her ear: "*Ammaa!* My mother has asked for *Sawaa Rupayaa!* My school fee is due! Today is the last date. My name will be struck off the register if not paid today!"

This temerity – psychic practice – after having done this I stepped aside, noticing embarrassingly that the family members congregated around the rope-cot of the grandee had started deriding me, laughing and mocking and jeering at me. Some of them did deride me too commenting, "Why, *eh*, are you up to detach our grandma's ears?"

After all, the grandee was large-hearted and broad-minded just like her grand personality. Beckoning to one of her daughters-in-law, she commanded, "Lo, what is he saying? Probably asking for something! Give him *Sawaa Rupayaa* by picking up from the niche there!" Then addressing me she uttered, "In which class do you read, *Eh*?"

"In class six, section B, *Ammaa!*"

The assembled lot broke into laughter once again.

"Oh well, very good! You are very brilliant *Eh*! Do study all the more sincerely and intensively!"

And no sooner had I got the begged amount in my little palms than I vaulted like a fawn towards my mother's dwelling whatever it was; and on the rear of me I heard an uproar: 'Oh, Oh, he has fled! He has made away with *Sawaa Rupayaa!* Thief! Thief! Hold him! Catch him!'

Felt like I had won the battle of life – the *Mahaabhaarat,* like I had won the gamble of education! Mother was ebullient, too, at this critical success. I did as if got rid of all the anxieties for life with the acquisition of the rupee and a quarter! Merely 125 *paise*!

Yet on the same day in the morning only, as soon as the school started and the class teacher entered the class, he without any fact checking of the current status started upbraiding me obliterating all my hopes and sweet fancies for the day, "Today is the deadline when your name will be struck off! From tomorrow onward, you need not come to school! You will learn a fitting lesson this way! You cannot bring *Sawaa Rupayaa* from your home!"

I with the rupee and a quarter in my hand, in my fist, tried in vain to make him see the reality, the pelf, but the salesman of education was as though hell bent upon playing his recorded tape that he had predisposed against me, the small kid.

I kept standing there as a mute spectator of his unwarranted tyranny and prejudice towards me, feeling humiliated beyond measure, thinking 'these chaps will think me a wretch!' To be called or considered a wretch or a poor person is a very despicable proposition! In this world, in this society, everybody is instructed as well as educated to look down upon the poor, the wretches, the resourceless and the money-less. And who is the soul who would like to be looked down upon by anybody!

Sort of strewing or throwing the fees onto the table of the class-teacher I had stood there with my head held high, full of self-esteem –

along with an enraged reticent cry in my child's heart. The clouds of humiliation intended to precipitate through the tears from my small and lovely eyes, musing all the more that I was subject to this undeserved contempt without any fault of mine on my part, a small innocent child! As for me, I had arranged the fees by exerting to the full, paying the heavy price of suffering the humiliation before my playmates. That happiness that I had gained in the wake of my success in arranging a rupee and a quarter in the morning, the insensitive salesman of instructions, greedy for fees, had crushed callously allegorically alike the cruelty of a butcher.

"Oh, you are up with the fees this time! Then no need to strike off your name!" Emerging as it did from the mouth of the class teacher was this voice assuaging me in a faked manner, peeking at me as though from below the eyes ensconced behind the specs of a mouse.

"Do listen attentively! The teacher is *shaitaan*! The father is *shaitaan*! The mother is *shaitaan*, too!", I responded to the query of *Mahaarathee*.

*Mahaarathee*, however, did burst into laughter but foolishly, alike a buffoon; he didn't know how to laugh and least of all, when. The teacher was not to miss this breach of serenity; his eyes got fixed oozing out a stream of fire from them onto the childish *Mahaarathee*: "Who is the scoundrel who is making a noise?"

I too uttered trying to check my intriguing laughter, "*Aachaaryajee*, I am trying to make him comprehend the import of these proverbs!"

"Well, well! Very good! Do it! This duffer is hard to teach, nothing enters his skull easily! Lo, how foolishly he has been splitting in the class!"

'*Hm hm hm hm.....*' baring his dirty teeth *Mahaarathee* was seen laughing like a foolhardy guy; his laughter had overpowered him as if, having taken control of his dwarfed soul!

XXX



## 20. *Melodious Calling*

*Enter protagonist*

"*Arvind!*"

This voice! This melodious calling! As though in the lively coolness of the dawn a musical note had been resonating, as if the music itself got personified!

Even today within my breaths, within my mind, within my cerebrum, or within my memory, I am listening the same musical note – the reiteration of the same sweet voice: ceaselessly! Whenever I happen to contemplate, I happen to hear the echo of the same voice, the same sweet voice: "*Arvind!*" It has not gone silent over the years and decades; even after the lapse of half a century!

Looking for the source of this divine sonority, the musical sound, my adolescent eyes did start glinting all of a sudden alike those of a fawn – the baby of a deer; expectantly! Just now, for the first time in my life, I had experienced the novel thrill of wading through the water canal – the *Gangaa Nahar* - which had merely ankle deep level of water in it, with little flow or velocity of currents. Nevertheless, side by side a fear did lurk in my heart, too, thinking that if the same terrific torrents of the water - which were seen during the full level of the canal - did come rushing towards us without warning when we were midway the stream, what would be our fate! It would be definite death! Nothing but death! Of course, this was not the first day of my going to the school! I had already taken admission in class six in this school, and had been there for many months. First terminal exams had passed, the summers had gone and the winter had set in. Nevertheless, this was my first occasion to go this way to school, particularly, by crossing the canal when it had little or no water, wading through the ankle-deep water.

This was the age when I had the impression that the tree of my life was an immortal entity, when I had the conception that my life would become a flower from the bud, and from flower it would become a blossom, and then assume the shape of a great bouquet, and so on....! Possibly I had given up when it came to thinking beyond the bounds of consciousness, or by the yond of normal senses: I found myself helpless to think beyond the 'and so on....'! My mind – my adolescent consciousness -- by then was not willing to accept any limits to the development, the growth – the development as well as flourishing of the phenomenon of life. That's why I had exclaimed on one such occasion to one of my fellow commuters as well as my companion to the school, "After class six, there would be class seven! After seven, there would be class eight! And after eight, nine! ..... and twenty, twenty one....", and so on....

The playmate was somewhat elder to me, possibly more intelligent, more worldly, much earthly than I was; he retorted: "After sixteen, there's no class anymore!"

"Then? What's then thereafter?"

Overwhelming the sweet if only crazy curiosity of mine so as to find an answer to this intractable and mystical question, there did arise as if from nowhere this melodious musical note: *'Arvind!'*

From the lips of *Raajeshwaree!* I saw: with hands upraised, attired in decent pinkish raiment, an adolescent girl of likely ten or eleven, with her specially thin and seductive lips, was letting escape this musical tone from her lovely lips: *'Arvind!'*

Afar there on that upraised hummock of mud outside the house that was perched thereupon, where she was standing with her satchel slung on her slender shoulders, possibly there were some other girls, too – all her friends – waiting for their school-fellow – all but students of lower grades like that of mine – class six!

This was the age for me when I didn't like my name being called or hailed by someone, particularly, not by an adolescent girl like that, in that manner, in front of one and all, my playmates, my companions from the village. 'Who is she in relation to me who dares to evoke my name like this, gesticulating and beckoning to me, using her hands? *Maan na maan, Main teraa mehmaan!* (Welcome or not, I am still your guest!)'

My companion nonetheless came to my rescue and did assuage my hurt sensibly by commenting, rather counselling, "Crazy as she maybe, do continue you, walking without a word in response!" He was possibly having a better sense of girlish affairs, which I didn't

have. I could only think that the boys ought to have no truck with girls, and men ought to have nothing to do with women! In fact I was given that sort of an injunction during my societal upbringing so far.

Anyway, leaving all that aside, presently I am intending to take you to *Raajeshwaree.* She was in fact the exceptionally enchanting lass of the class in which descended the elves like *Shakuntalaa, Urvashee, Menakaa, Rambhaa, Raadhaa,* or, the other ones, if there be any other allegories or metaphors for the highest measurements of feminine beauty and glamour in the cosmos. The other day when she hailed me from afar as *'Arvind'* she did actually sweep away or drive away from my heart or mind the phenomenon of strangeness between me and herself. After that day, too, she had never flinched from teasing me or, so to say, from embarrassing me even for a moment or on a single day. Now what should I reminisce and what I should skip out of what did happen between her and myself! Almost everything was on her part! Nothing from my side except trying my best to maintain a detached distance from them – hers and her other two classmates, my classmates as well! How far a lass can go or how long a rope can an adolescent girl take in dealing with a handsome and chubby, cherub, lad of her age and grade! What mischiefs they did not do to entrap me or to make me be on talking terms with them! However, I was a shy guy, ever scared of the company of opposite sex, fair sex, of girls.

Yet, at least one cause, one puzzle, I find myself to sort out is that I can claim on oath of anything that I was not the most handsome, healthy or seductive lad of the class – as has been corroborated by my wife in later life after my marriage to her, that I am none of a handsome man – yet why was it that *Raajeshwaree* was so much enamoured of me, so much attracted towards me? One cause but I can guess is that I was the most gifted as well as brilliant student of the class. By that time, in the first quarterly exam it was me who had scored the highest marks in the class. And later on, too, it was me only who kept on standing first in the class. And I feel, the wisdom adds an additional feather to the cap, an additional amount of aura and glamour to a human being!

However, good marks I had scored in classes four and five, too! Yeah! But hadn't the beautiful, pretty girls started loving me there too! Of course, in class five, when I was reprimanded, or slapped in the face, on the very first day of that school, my mind got utterly upset. The loyalty and reverence that ought to have been shown and harboured in heart towards that salesman of education – the solo master - had forsaken me the very first day. I think it was good. Unless one intends to be fooled into believing otherwise at the hands of the salesman, a lingering feeling must go on in the heart that the salesman is looting; every salesman sees one's interest first, and the consumer sees his interest first!

XXX



## 27. Providential Mix-up
*Enter protagonist*

Let me tell you yet another incident that deepens the belief of *'Aachaarya Shaitaano Bhava!'*. The result of class 6 examination came out. I went to school with great enthusiasm. I had hoped that I would get the first place, as well as get the highest marks in all the subjects. The result card came in my hands; I found that I got the first place. I was very happy. But seeing the mark sheet, I was surprised that in English, I got only 64 marks out of 120, while I was thinking that I would have got more than 100 marks. At the same time, I saw the boy next to me in roll call being very happy: he had scored 98 marks, while he was a *Buddhoo* – mediocre - boy in the class. He was hopping around pronouncing to boys, 'I have scored more marks in English than *Arvind* has!' This conundrum, this unbelievable and unexpected occurrence I could not resolve at that juncture. Nevertheless, I apprehended that while making the mark-sheet, my marks might have been entered in the mark-sheet of that boy and my marks onto his mark-sheet.

But I could not muster the courage to go to the teacher and express this doubt to the teachers, because I was always fed with the input: 'Be always scared! Don't argue with anyone! Even when you are in the right! Don't resist even the injustice being done to you or others!'

The parental precepts proffered to me were but those befitting the cowards and slaves, or those that could produce only a coward and a slave of bullies.

XXX



## 28. Fire-Wood Cutter
*Enter protagonist*

The year passed off smoothly and fortunately for me for I had regained or retained my reputation as a gifted lad in the school and in the village. My reputation was so high that wherever and whenever I passed by, the parents and grandparents of children beckoned to their wards pointing out that it was me who was a prodigy. Of course, this filled my heart with gratification, but not pride. On the contrary, I felt lack of privacy in such situations. In such an onslaught of praise and admiration I started hating the 'praise' itself, the fame itself. I was a famous prodigy, sort of. I found myself praying to God to rid me of my fame and popularity, for it was suffocating in a sense. How precious the anonymity is I could realise in that glaring and glittering situation only.

However gifted or famous I might have been in the eyes of school mates, or teachers, or the villagers, my lot was not enviable at home. Our financial condition had soon started showing its weakness. The firewood had been exhausted fully. The food-grains had always been in short supply. My mother was somehow managing the household on the strength of whatever little money she had brought from her parents, of course, collected over the foregone year when she had been living in exile there. Father himself was short of funds. Living at a far off village, that too, along with the relatives, drawing a petty salary of hardly two hundred rupees per month, he could not afford to pay anything to us, as now I realise in hind sight. For, by the turn of the year when it was approaching harvest time, I found my mother quite constrained for money. She had to beg for even small sums from the villagers. Whenever she borrowed money from someone she had to take help of *Lakshmee* – the wife of a barber –

who was a kind-hearted lady and managed debts at usury on behalf of usurers in the village. However extortionist it might feel – for the rate of interest charged for these borrowings at times would be 48 or 60 percent per annum, that too, compoundable at half yearly rests – the borrowers felt obliged, for they did get the most required commodity, the money promptly.

When the harvest season approached, my mother saw that the soft stalks of the mustard plants that were grown in the fields on the banquettes of the agricultural beds were standing all alone there in the fields around our homestead. Our homestead was having its door towards the fields, so we could notice them. The firewood was always in short supply for my poor mother. She had to arrange two meals for her three kids, and that too she was finding extremely tough.

She suggested to me, her eleven year old son, supposedly a gifted prodigy of the area, to exert in those fields and cut the mustard stalks for using as firewood. I obeyed my mother happily, and also, I felt pleasure in doing that job. It used to be hot and sultry in the fields at times but I used the evening hours when the sunrays were slanted and the sun felt lesser ferocious in intensity. The owners of the fields would see me exerting in the empty fields and those who did know me

would say nothing, that is, would not object to my cutting the fire-woods from their fields. However, those who could not recognise me, they thought that I might be some lower caste chap cutting fire-woods from their fields, their property, and they would definitely raise objection and hue and cry, even upbraiding me like a lower caste poor person. It was a fashion to create hindrance in the living of lower caste poor people even when there was no need to do so. Then I had to clarify that I was the son of so and so, thinking that my father's was some great name and everybody would respect that and allow me to take away the wood stalks. It was not true; my father was nothing in the eyes of sensible villagers, for he was resourceless, my father contemplating that he himself was a gun notwithstanding. Normally I succeeded in collecting ample amount of firewood for my mother despite all these setbacks, humiliations and hindrances.

But one day my cousin – *Yuvraaj* – who was kind-hearted as well as seasoned, approached me in the agricultural field itself when I was cutting the soft stalks of the mustard plants and warned me thus, "You are wasting your precious time and labour in cutting woods whereas being a brilliant student you are supposed to take care of your health, eyes and brain." He said many more things, and now in the hindsight I realise that he would have been sent by my aunt – her mother – who was an educated lady unlike my own mother who did not have the considerations like my cousin or his mother had. I felt somewhat perplexed as well as disheartened after this counsel by my cousin. And at that moment I realised that what I was doing was not a very noble task; it was befitting the lower strata of society in fact. That my parents could not afford even firewood living as they did in a village, owning fifteen *beeghaas* of arable land, was itself a reflection on their level of skills or lack of it.

After my cousin had cautioned me I started doubting what was told about my family and parents, that they hailed from a good or great *khaandaan.* I started taking pity on myself; I became prey to the feeling of self-pity: I was such a wretched son of worthless couple!

However, I could not help it. When I brought this fact to the notice of my mother, my mother brushed aside the idea of my cousin, saying what the harm was there in collecting firewood from the fields standing just in front of us. We lacked fuel wood and we were collecting it. They did not need it, for they did not lack it. So far so good! I was satisfied, convinced, but in my heart I developed an inferiority complex that despite being the brightest guy of the school

and the most famous lad of the village I was destined to be just a poor wretched labourer, rather, a wood-cutter in my family, and that there was no consideration for my giftedness in my family's eyes. Even in the eyes of Providence! My sisters were too young and they could not come to my rescue, however.

Also at times, I thought what the greatness or *khaandaaniyat* of my grandfather or the pedigree meant for me when I was obliged to live in such dire straits! All sham greatness! Simply a mockery of the term greatness or riches!

XXX



## 29. Alcoholism And Devastation, Thy Name Is Feudalism

*Enter father*

In the field of millets where we were weeding out the undergrowth amidst the stench of night soil, my son further asked me about the visit of one of our cousins from *Ajmer* where the latter's father had settled.

Before even narrating the intriguing tale, a few words towards introduction of the actors of this tale!

In fact, in our broader family tree, this particular sibling had settled at *Ajmer* where he used to serve in Railways most likely. His wife settled as she was in the urban environs, that is, away from the village folks, thus immune from the obligations of relationships, chose to keep herself secluded from the village folks; so that she could avert the demands of the relatives on the pocket of her husband. She deliberately behaved abrasively with whosoever visited them at their place so that, once humiliated, the relatives would never think of revisiting them in future. This was her deliberate tactics – a shrewdness – to guard her forte for her own selfish sake. She had become a butt of joke and derision in our family circle amongst the elder people, like, my father and *Chhote Daadaa* etc; the latter called her by the appellation *'Kalaawatee Bhaabhee'*, and this was used in derisive sense to denote a person who is utterly selfish, self-centred as well as money-minded, and who does not care for one's relationships. She was not *'Kalaawatee Bhaabhee'* for us second generation lads; for us she was *'Kalaawatee Taaee'* and for the next generation to us, that is, for our son's generation, she was *'Kalaawatee Ammaa'*. It is not that her name was only a matter of derision, there were also her votaries, supporters who praised her attitude towards rustic villagers. For instance, our *Bhaabhee* – the wife of our elder cousin who also served in Railways at *Ajmer* only – was all praise for the virtues of *Kalaawatee Taaee*; she could not tolerate a word

against the old lady, for she herself was like her only in demeanour. However, the junior lady did not get any derisive appellations, or if she did, I do not know; that might be confined to the talks of next generation.

I have noticed that those who have the good luck of deserting their motherland and the poor villagers, think themselves to be worthy of that good fortune and only themselves to be performers of noble deeds. And in the process they start denigrating the poor innocent villagers and leave them to their wretched fates.

This *Kalaawatee Taaee* of ours had four sons apart from daughters whatever number thereof she might have had, and her husband had already passed away at the time when we were conversing in the millet field. Ours being a family having an old regal legacy, one of her sons was wedded to one of the princesses of the royal family of *Chhaataa, Teekamgarh,* though there was nothing princely in the personality or beauty of the lady. She was a normal face. Actually, in the name of royal family there lived a large retinue of women folks who work as menial staff or as sex workers for the large set up of the royal family, and all of them claim themselves to be the princesses or queens; they were actually slaves or workers. And the prince or the king used to be benevolent enough to arrange their marriages in good families by giving the latter his name as well as prestige. And no doubt that was a good gesture!

As the fate would have it, none of the four sons of the aunt was settled properly; all were boozers, alcoholics, womanisers *et al*. That was nothing unusual, however. Everybody expected at least that much regality from every member of the feudal set ups! In the absence of such vices one was not considered a blue blooded feudal person, rather.

One of my maternal uncle's daughters was also married to one of her sons; and she was never happy thereafter. She lived a wretched life; might be cursing me, for it was I who had managed this nuptial bond.

One of *Kalaawatee Taaee's* sons was an addict of liquor, and badly addicted one. After the death of his father, that is, *Kalaawatee Taaee's* husband, he started visiting the village, our village, their ancestral village.

"Why?" queried my son.

"They had got a large swathe of arable land to their father's share in the large inheritance here; and he wanted to dispose that of. He and his family had no source of income anymore, their earning father having died already, and the family pension being hardly enough for the *Taaee's* sustenance.

"None of them got any job?"

"None!"

"Alike you!" chuckled my son.

I got shocked at this low appraisal of my worth, nonetheless, I kept mum.

"They were all proclaimed bullies of *Ajmer – Raamganj mauhalla*. Their eldest brother was a known name in the colony, a respectable notoriety in fact: *Raajoo Daadaa!* And he was ever on the loggerheads with the youths of another clan in the college: *Jaats.*"

"For what?"

"For no cause, of course! Simply for emulating the bravado being shown in the movies and talkies those days!"

"Okay, let's come back to our story…"

"Yeah, the tale of your cousin's visit to our village that summer, and your giving company to him all the time, to my utter amazement. He was a drunkard, and you were treating him as if he were your best chum…." Added my son truthfully.

"Yes, that's true! That summer he stayed here for long; not only summer, during the preceding winter as well he had been to the village negotiating for the sale of their share of land. During summer, of course, he stayed here without a break."

"But why were you accompanying him all the time, despite knowing fully well that he was a bad man, a drunkard…?"

"Actually, I did not want to remain in his company, but he was ever so insistent. Moreover, having spent all his little money, the cash, whatever he was in possession of, he was always demanding money from me, also not letting me go."

"Strange! But where was he eating?"

"His close relatives here had exhausted their patience in feeding him regularly and they had now stopped even asking him for food; he was therefore relying on me only for filling his belly."

"But you yourself didn't have food even to fill the bellies of your wretched family!"

At this I expressed my annoyance; I could not take this umbrage on my son's part alleging me of indolence. However, my son was unrepentant in his conviction that I was an indolent person. Now he also seemed to be in the know of my being a drunkard, an alcoholic addict myself.

He further added, "For months together, you both were seen together loitering around aimlessly, doing nothing, seemingly only boozing and loafing around in the hamlet, to my bewilderment. I considered you to be an ascetic before that, given your sham sermons given to me. But there were days when you created ruckus in our little home demanding good food for you both, even as, you had arranged no wherewithal for that. You used to be seen badly intoxicated, to my utter shock. In that state, you even had an altercation – a foul one – with even your younger sister. She also used the words unbecoming of hers, or those that did not fit into the close relationship of a brother and sister at least. At that juncture, I had a shocking realisation that the relationships are just sham, that those have no sanctity, and that they are based on one's own self-interests, and can be thrown to dogs if one's own selfish ends were not met…."

My son would have continued, however, I interjected, "I did not like that drunkard, but I could not help it…."

"What finally happened to his nefarious mission of disposing of family inheritance of prestigious arable land, the land for which erstwhile ancestors could let their heads roll?"

"It was not settled yet."

"Why?"

"For there were no buyers. Let me tell you, in a rural set-up, it is not easy to sell the agricultural land. Nobody considers it honourable to sell one's land; it is tantamount to selling one's honour forever. However, those spoilt brats who have settled in towns and urban environs do not harbour any such notions; for them, instant gratification is everything. They do not consider land as their mother, or a matter of prestige and honour for their pedigree."

"So, nobody in the village ventured to accept their land, despite being capable of doing so!"

"Yeah, for there is yet another aspect to it, too; that is, the purchaser of anybody's land is taken to be an implied enemy or adversary of the relatives of the seller. And at times the sale culminates even in settling of scores through murder or burning of one's barns, as it happened in this case, as you know."

"Yes, that was really awful and heart-wrenching!"

"But that tale at some other time, for that happened two years later when these brats were able to convince someone from our broad family circle only to buy their portion of land; and the relatives of sellers set fire to the whole stock of harvest piled up in the buyers' barns, as you know!"

"Yes, indeed! World and specially human society is so weird!"

The world was much weirder than what my son was surmising, I thought.

XXX



## 30. Beginning Of The End-Game

*Enter protagonist*

While staying at my maternal relatives' abode the year before, I had formed a conviction that whoever was living or was present there would remain there as such forever, that there would be no change ever in the milieu obtaining there, not only as regards human beings, but also, other sub-human creatures as well as cattle, birds and beasts. Childish fancy!

Despite there being the constant flow and show of unstoppable change and disappearance of scenes from the arena of eyes, we as children could not discern the phenomenon of ephemerality of everything that pervades the entire Creation, the entire universe. Save the crops and seasons which kept on changing constantly we could not notice anything that was changing in that tiny habitat, at least during that one year.

At the end of the academic session at my paternal village, when we were planning to pack off to our *Nanihaal*, our benefactors – our elder uncle and aunt along with their retinue of half a dozen children - were visiting our village, rather, their home at their village. As already told, we were simply staying in their shelter home as refugees. The entire lot of two families were scheduled to go to *Nanihaal* in a day or two.

Suddenly and unexpectedly, we kids noticed that our younger *Maamaajee* had come to our village. We got very happy to see such a suave person as our younger *maamaa*. We thought at first that he had come just like our aunt and uncle had come to visit us at the end of the session.

However, we overheard our aunt remark to our *maamaajee*, "So, *bade baabaa* is gone?" (So, the elder uncle has passed away?)

In remarking this sorrowful fact her countenance in fact did not betray any signs of grief or sorrow which is normally felt at the countenances of relatives whose dear ones have departed. My elder aunt was of that nature; she seldom mourned anybody's death. She harboured the notion however that she was immortal and that the death, the ubiquitous phenomenon of dying was applicable merely to others, other than herself and her family. That notion persisted with her for quite a while until she suffered her first bereavement at the death of her youngest daughter who had committed suicide following a failed love affair which had resulted in premarital pregnancy by a tenant who was staying with them at the city of *Ajmer*.

*Bade baabaa* means our elder *Naanaajee*, in fact, the elder cousin of our *Naanaajee*. He had dubbed me a *'Bhonpoo'* (loud-speaker) when I was a crying baby in my babyhood. He used to discipline the vendors of vegetables and other wares thereby checking their cheating of peasants. Against whom my mother had the recurring complaint that he put so many restrictions on the girls of his household as regards outing and mixing up with the opposite sex. My mother asserted that as against *Bade Baabaa's* demeanour her own father, that is, my *Naanaajee* was a liberal person in this behalf; he is reported to have no such apprehensions about her girls mixing up with lads. And my mother was pleased to have such a father! She also did not mince words to praise her father for this special trait of his. My mother I had heard umpteen number of times complaining that *Bade Baabaa* was a very suspicious type of person, that he suspected the adolescent and young girls about the latter's activities. Obviously, my mother was hinting at something connected with sensuousness associated with young lasses and lads. She also averred that whereas she herself used to roam around the village unrestricted and could lord over even the lads of the small hamlet, her cousin – who was incidentally also married in the same family fold as my mother, however, to a senior man, owing to her higher age – was never allowed by *Bade Baabaa* to roam around in the village. Now, who was right and who wrong, I have never been able to decide yet.

The same *Bade Naanaajee* had passed away. When my *maamaajee* conveyed this message to our mother and elder aunt – his sisters – I could little realise that our elder *Naanaajee* would no more be available for interaction on this planet or anywhere anymore. I simply surmised that the death was also a happening like any other incidents taking place in this universe.

However, that was not true; *Bade Naanaajee* had disappeared for good. This depressing realisation dawned upon me when we reached the *Nanihaal* a day or two after that and found the visitors wailing and crying for the death of the old man. An irreversible happening had taken place, I realised.

There only, I came to know that our elder *maamaajee* had become utterly upset with the death of his elder uncle. He could be consoled after much effort on the part of village elders. I was amazed to learn this, for I thought that our elder *maamaajee* was a tough-minded man and that he would not be impacted by such incidents as death of the near and dear ones. However, that was not true. His elder uncle's death proved to be an eye opening experience for him. I heard him narrate his trauma in this regard to the family barber who had come to shave the family elders in the wake of the death in the family. My *maamaajee* was lamenting to the barber – the servant – that *Bade Baabaa* would be seen no more, that he felt like getting chocked to think that *Bade Baabaa* would never be seen on this earth now.

I being a child, did not mind this grave realisation too much, yet at least one thing was there that I realised that the chain of the phenomenon of disappearance of living souls had started, that one by one every elder would disappear, and that this was only a matter of a few years. And that was true. However young we may be, the time is not far when we would be the next person in queue, when death would claim us, too. Definitely and decidedly!

XXX



**The End**

## English Books by *'Videh'*

*Hypocrisy & Reality* (fiction series: 9 books)

**'Hypocrisy & Reality'** is a fiction series comprising multiple books – novels. The fiction is aimed at depicting the hypocrisy of human society in every respect, be it the upbringing and treatment of babies, toddlers, children, adolescents, youths, or be it the treatment meted out to adults, aged ones, those who are closely related with oneself, with one's blood; not to speak of those called strangers or outsiders. Barring a rarity, nobody cares two hoots for the sentiments or security and safety of other living creatures on this sole planet nurturing 'living' beings!

*Book 1: Beyond the Pale* (fiction)

**'Beyond the Pale'** of Time & Space is the first volume of the long fiction series 'Hypocrisy & Reality' and as the name suggests, it deals with the timespan in the life of the protagonist when one had not even had a tryst with the concepts of Time and Space, nor did they make any difference in one's life if those ubiquitous phenomena were not taken cognizance of. Those were the years before the realm of schooling, the arena of perfect unconcern for the written letters, words, or numbers.

*Book 2: Wilderness of Literacy* (fiction)

**'Wilderness of Literacy'** is the second volume in the long fiction series 'Hypocrisy & Reality' and, as the name suggests, it takes the protagonist in the arena of letters, words, and numbers: the realm of what we call the 'literacy'. The experience of a child while treading this seemingly dreaded as well as untrodden landscape is nothing short of venturing into a wilderness; of course, led and mentored first by one's parents and thereafter invariably by their preceptors -- the masters -- all of whom have a tremendous amount of impact on the future human being that emerges from their inputs given and endeavours made towards making a man, the humanity.

*Book 3: Advent of Time* (fiction)

**'Advent of Time'** is the third volume in the long fiction series entitled 'Hypocrisy & Reality' and covers the schooling period when the protagonist discovered the phenomenon of Time, and also, figuratively he felt that it was then his time, even as, he mysteriously discovered his latent potential and wisdom catapulting himself into the uppermost orbits of glory, fame and all round applause from his classmates, masters as well as teachers. To his own amazement as well as bewilderment! Nevertheless, this providential blessing was not without its blemishes in the shape of rancour and envy of fellow classmates and their patrons towards him. Even as, Nature never allows anybody pleasure and praise without at the same time associating with them the equivalent amount of pain and back-biting!

*Book 4: Devoid of Shelter* (fiction)

**'Devoid of Shelter'**, the fourth volume in the long fiction series 'Hypocrisy & Reality' furthers the journey of the protagonist into the world where he discovered to his dismay that he had no place on the globe which he could call as his home; he had no place of his own where he could take shelter during the day, and during the night. He somehow made do with seeking shelter with the relatives – maternal chiefly; not as a transitory phenomenon, but for good, until he himself took command of his life, snatching himself away from the indolent lifestyle of his parents. He also discovered during the refuge that however meritorious one might be, without the good base of ancestry, one was not considered as such.

### Book 5: Price of Refuge (fiction)

'**Price of Refuge**', the fifth volume in the fiction series 'Hypocrisy & Reality' furthers the journey of the protagonist into the world when he returned to his paternal relatives and found to his dismay that his father was absolutely incapable of arranging a dwelling of his own. Also, he found himself to be a mute subject to child abuse at the hands of none other than supposedly an elder cousin of his, the son of his so-called benefactors who provided refuge in their vacant house. That was the price paid by the child for the indolence and handicaps of an unworthy father for seeking shelter under the tutelage of so-called relatives. No refuge seemingly looking innocuous goes without some price to be paid either by self, spouse or one's children.

### Book 6: Hatred towards Love (fiction)

'**Hatred towards Love**', the sixth volume in the fiction series 'Hypocrisy & Reality' furthers the journey of the protagonist into the world where to his amusement he found himself catapulted into the realm of a celebrity or at least a child prodigy as far as the small rural catchment area was concerned. By virtue of his giftedness in the realm of studies and his bewitching countenance, the classmates, especially, the lasses of her age could not help restraining themselves from loving him; and they did it overtly, without caring for the opinions and feelings of other class-fellows. Albeit the protagonist himself wallowed in the faulty ideology that having any truck with fair sex was anathema and a great sin which could not be washed away in later life.

### Book 7: Towards the Yoga (fiction)

'**Towards the Yoga**', the seventh volume in the fiction series 'Hypocrisy & Reality' dwells on the period in the journey of life of the protagonist when he was at the pinnacle of his bodily prowess and psychic acuity, thanks to his habit of pursuing *Yogaasans* regularly as well as religiously. As though something divine was associated with the pursuit of *Yogaasans*, his father luckily could get an *ad hoc* teacher's job in the town school too; however, that was not to be sustained throughout for at the fag-end of the academic session, his father fell out with the Principal of school and was expelled. *Yoga,* nevertheless, gave the protagonist a hue that was unparallelled, and which materialised into the worldly as well as societal fame for him.

### Book 8: On the Descent (fiction)

'**On the Descent**', the eighth volume in the fiction series 'Hypocrisy & Reality' takes the protagonist over the hump. He was then a ward of such a guardian who did not have any wherewithal to run his household, yet had no qualms about begetting more issues, more and more at that. Agriculture, of course, he had as an inheritance but he was by nature averse to anything even distantly associated with agriculture or Nature, for that matter. Any industrious as well as expedient agriculturalist would have eked out one's livelihood quite easily from the fifteen *beeghaa*s of arable land his father had inherited from his resourceful, brave as well as powerful ancestors, but not he.

### *Book 9: In the Exile* (fiction)

**'In the Exile'**, the ninth volume in the fiction series 'Hypocrisy & Reality' furthers the journey of the protagonist into the world where post his dramatic jump into the orbit of fame in the wake of his High School result, he found himself entirely in a barren land where he could see no ray of hope from his father, even as, the latter was totally incapable of arranging the means to further the studies for his exceptionally gifted son. For the first time, the protagonist realised that his father was incapable of meeting his requirements for pursuing further studies. He was already suffering emotionally having been separated from his mother for the first time! This was for him like an exile, that too, very uncomfortable!

### *Bewailing Muse* (poetry)

Be it the sage *Valmeeki* or be it the modern poet *Sumitraa Nandan Pant*, both have held that poetry has its founts in heart and is the outcome of extreme sorrow, misery or pangs of separation. Poetry cannot be created; it gets engendered out of compulsion. From the heart! Heart's language is poetry or musing! I have offered to christen them as Muse: 'Bewailing Muse'; the first musings out of wailings! Nevertheless, I am tempted not to treat them as children's literature for I sense some

substantial element, too, in them. The period of the composition of these poems is from 1972 to 1976; and I feel that my wailings have not fallen on deaf ears, so to say, given my present circumstances of life which are totally opposite to the then prevailing ones!

### *Chambellion* (drama: comedietta)

In the genre of Drama (Comedietta), here is the playlet *'Chambellion'* that exposes the bizarre reality of the political developments post transfer of reins from the whites to the yellow people in the guise of 'Democracy' and 'Independence'; whereas actually the latter have been pursuing their dynastic agenda and propagating their own family fiefdoms that have flourished like weeds in multitudes in the void created by annihilation of Princely states and Landlords. Allegorically, it may be compared with the weed flourishing in an agricultural field which has remained unsown after harvest of the previous crop. For the subjects, verily, there is no Freedom whatsoever, in literal sense.

### *Brainy Beasts* (short stories)

This is an anthology of short stories, included wherein are four short stories or farces, so to say, that is, anecdotes including the 'In An Illegible Script', which is the English version of the author's *Hindee* short story *'Anpadh Lipi Mein...* (अनपढ़ लिपि में)' that was first published in now extinct though the then prestigious *Hindee* magazine the *'Kaadambinee'* way back in July, 1992, with quite an applause and accolades from the sides of kind readers! Other stories or anecdotes are also those published in other places, i.e. journals of variegated hues. Nothing uttered in these works is meaningless; this conviction is at work behind the inspiration to publish them in book form for kind readers.

***Search for Life*** (translation of 'Hatyaaree Sadee Mein Jeevan Kee Khoj' (हत्यारी सदी में जीवन की खोज))
English Translation by *'Videh' Arvind Kumar* of *Hindee* poetry book *'Hatyaaree Sadee Mein Jeevan Kee Khoj' (हत्यारी सदी में जीवन की खोज)* by renowned young poet *'Nirvikaar' Mukesh Kumar*. This book has earned *'Nirvikaar'* the award of *'Jai Shankar Prasaad Puraskaar'* of Rs. One Lac from the *'Rajya Karmchaaree Saahitya Sansthaan, Uttar Pradesh'*. On the *Hindee* book *'Hatyaaree Sadee Mein Jeevan Kee Khoj,'* critiques by renowned personalities -- both young and old -- like *Ashwaghosh, Prempaal Sharmaa, Rajeev Saxena, Dr Anoop Singh, Dr Devkee Nandan Sharmaa, Manoj Kumaar Jhaa, Gautam Rajarshi,* etc have been published in various journals and magazines. The renowned critic Dr *Om Nishchal* has included this anthology in the select category for *'Kavya Paridrishya'* of 2017 amongst the famous poetry books.

***Reality of Invisible*** (translation of 'Adrishya Kaa Yathaarth' (अदृश्य का यथार्थ))
English translation by *'Videh' Arvind Kumar* of the *Hindee* poetry book *'Adrishya Kaa Yathaarth' (अदृश्य का यथार्थ)* by renowned poet *'Ashwaghosh' Om Prakaash Sharmaa*. *'Ashwaghosh'* -- a well-known moniker of *Hindee*

world! A litterateur of impeccable renown! Praised by multitudes -- both in literary and plebeian spheres! He has been composing prolifically -- having published over two dozen books spanning all the genre! The thesis, the short stories, the short epics, the anthologies, the new genre songs, the *ghazals*, the poetry for children *et al*. Covering all age groups! He has been honoured with many awards in literary and academic fields by prestigious institutions.

***Nagasaki: Bomb & Aftermath*** (commentary on the first novel of Nobel Laureate, Kazuo Ishiguro) (Displayed on Oxford bookstore)
This is a work of literary study into the first novel 'The Pale View of Hills' by 2017 Literature Nobel Laureate, Kazuo Ishiguro, who has narrated in a mesmerising style of story telling the tale of Japanese society undergoing change in the aftermath of dropping of atomic bomb. The Americans not only vanquished and occupied the Japanese military and land by dropping the most lethal weapon never before heard of – the atomic bomb – on two of the Japanese cities, one of which was Nagasaki which witnessed this technological devastation on 8th of August, 1945, but also, occupied the minds and hearts of Japanese youth, both men and women. The youth of Japan started decrying everything old and conventional including their erstwhile education system and the ideologies of patriotism and nationalism.

***Procreation, the Adorable*** (English summary of Shiv Puraan)

The *Shiva-ling* has ever been a matter of amazement and mystery for mankind. That something obscure is there behind the adoration of such a carnal symbol as *ling* irrespective of the same being that of a deity called *Shiva* has ever been lingering in my mind. Why should a large majority of population in this land – from north to south -- worship the genitals so openly, so brazenly? So reverently! *Shiva* is supposed to be a mythological persona, in existence too long back in time, who might have been the pioneer in realizing the spectacular qualities of *ling* and *yoni,* specifically, those of converting the *sthaavar* (the insensate) into *jangam* (the sensate) and those of creating the *satva-lok,* (conscious beings).

***Self-Styled Sovereign, the Judiciary*** (Dramatic deliberation on the state of judiciary)

This is in fact an academic deliberation on the functioning and reality of the judicial system prevalent in India post what they euphemistically call the 'Independence' or, literally, the *'Aazaadee'.* Whose Independence was it anyway? For whom? Except for the ruling class? The lawyers first, and then the hooligans of *Chambal.* Nonetheless, the judiciary of the free country turned out to be one step further than its new crop of leaders; they usurped the entire authority from the latter in subtle moves one after the other. In olden epochs, the autocratic *Sultaans* or *Baadshaahs* dispensed justice purely depending upon their whims and fancies, which were incidental to the moods and tantrums of the Sovereign. Historically as well, the Real Sovereign was the one who dispensed justice. The Judiciary in Indian Republic soon realised this and acted.

XXX

# 'विदेह' रचित हिंदी ग्रंथ

*अनपढ़ लिपि* (कहानी-संग्रह)

'विदेह' अरविन्द कुमार की आठ हिंदी कहानियों का संकलन! संकलन की पहली कहानी 'अनपढ लिपि में ...' जुलाई, 1992 में प्रतिष्ठित हिंदी पत्रिका 'कादंबिनी' में छपी थी। 'सिग्नेचर' भी स्वच्छता के प्रति सरकारी महकमे की विद्रूपात्मक मनोदशा का कड़वा चित्रण है। 'ताकि आप अपने पक्ष में रहें!' नये प्रकार के कर्मचारियों की मानसिकता को इंगित करती है। फिर फिर वही लोग' भेड़-बकरियों की तरह दुरुपयोग किये जा रहे जन-समुदाय के विषय में कहानी है। 'अपार्थाइड' : वस्तुतः तो, शक्तिशाली और निर्बल का भेद ही असली रंग-भेद है। 'नया वेद' 'आज़ादी' नाम से वही पारम्परिक पद्धति चतुराई-पूर्वक 'नया संविधान' के नाम से चलाये जाने की पोल-पट्टी खोलती है। 'पहली कमाई' कहानी का आख्यान कल्पना से भी अधिक विस्मयकारी है! 'भगवान को पैसा' समाज और सरकार दोनों ही की धन के प्रति जो दृष्टि है, उस पर तीखा व्यंग्य है।

*पाषाण-युग* (कहानी-संग्रह)

'विदेह' अरविन्द कुमार की सात हिंदी कहानियों का संकलन! संकलन की पहली कहानी 'ब्लॉक का पेड़' आज के समाज में क्षीण होते हुए आपसी

सौहार्द्र, एवं अजनबियों के प्रति बढ़ते अकारण वैमनस्य, को बिंबित करती हुई सच्चाई है। 'मेरी ज्ञाति' भारत में जातियों के हास्यास्पद 'प्रहसन' – फ़ार्स (farce) -- को चित्रित करके इसकी विद्रूपता को व्यंजित करती है। 'हिंदू-मुसलमान' साम्प्रदायिकता के प्रश्न को व्यक्तियों – दो घनिष्ठ मित्रों -- के स्तर पर परीक्षण करके देखती है। 'मुर्गबाज' समय की नब्ज पर हाथ रखने की कोशिश है। 'मंदिरों, मस्जिदों, गुरुद्वारों, गिरजाघरों में ...' साम्प्रदायिक कट्टरता की निर्थकता को व्यंजित करने के लिए है, जो मृत्यु के पर्दे के पीछे कितनी हास्यास्पद बन जाती है! ऐ अधर्मी!' आदमी की नश्ल को बदलने की नाहक कोशिश कही जा सकती है। 'राक्षस' इस नये शासन-प्रशासन में व्याप्त भ्रष्टाचार पर एक व्यंग्यात्मक टिप्पणी है, और बताती है कि राक्षस कोई कपोल-कल्पना नहीं है, बल्कि आज भी एक वास्तविकता है।

### *निसर्ग* (कहानी-संग्रह)

'विदेह' अरविन्द कुमार की सात हिंदी कहानियों का संकलन! संकलन की पहली कहानी 'मुलाक़ात एक बड़े लेखक से' एक बड़े लेखक और एक आम आदमी के जीवन के साम्य और अंतर दोनों को ही उजागर करती है। 'फाड़ी हुई कविता' एक ऐसे पति की व्यथा-कथा है, जो एक कवि एवं साहित्यकार भी है। 'नया साल' में कुछ भी नया नहीं होता, फिर भी सारी दुनिया किस कदर बाबली हुई रहती है। 'हितैषिणी' शादी जैसी संस्थाओं के पाखण्ड, फ़रेब एवं परम्पराओं से चिपकाव की विद्रूपता पर सशक्त प्रहार करती है। 'छोटे-से शरीर में क़ैदी' शिशुमन की विवशता को चित्रित करती है; वह पूरी तरह माँ-बाप की मूर्खताओं पर निर्भर रहने को विवश है। 'निसर्ग' एक रोमांटिक कहानी है। 'टूट-टूटकर गिरते सितारे' दिखाती है कि कैसे समाज अपने ही शिकंजे में फँसा रहकर ही परेशान होता रहता है!

### *आर्त-गान* (कविता-संग्रह)

'वियोगी होगा पहला कवि, आह से उपजा होगा गान
उमड़कर आँखों से चुपचाप, बही होगी कविता अनजान!'

(सुमित्रा नंदन पंत)
या
'मा निषाद त्वम् गम: प्रतिष्ठाम् शाश्वती समा:
यत् क्रौंच मिथुनादेकम् त्वम् वधी: काम मोहितम्!'
(महर्षि वाल्मीकि)

चाहे तो आदि कवि वाल्मीकि हों, चाहे फिर छायावादी कवि पंत हों, एक बात तो तय है, कि कविता वियोग या विषाद या शोक से उत्सृजित होती है। पहले-पहल की रचनाएँ हैं ये – जीवन के पहले-प्रहर की; अतः बच्चों के उपयुक्त ही हो सकती हैं। बाल-कविता! बाल-कविता इसे मैंने फिर भी इसलिए नहीं कहा है, क्योंकि इनमें मुझे कुछ सार भी सन्निहित लगता रहा है; एकदम तो बकवास नहीं ही हैं ये, जैसी कि बाल (अबोध) -कविता की प्रकृति और प्रवृत्ति होती है। ये कविताएँ 1972 से 1976 के काल-खंड में सृजित हैं; और अभी लगभग अर्ध-शती की परिपक्व दृष्टि से भी परिमार्जित!

### *काल-क्रंदन* (कविता-संग्रह)

जीवन के प्रथम प्रहर की हृदयाभिव्यक्तियों (1972 से 1976 तक) के 'आर्त-गान' के बाद, 1979 से 1990 तक के द्वादश वर्षीय काल-खण्ड में मैंने जो क्रंदन किया था, उसे मैने कविता कहा; और उन कविताओं का 'काल-रेख' नाम मैंने चुना था; क्योंकि काल की छाती पर 12 वर्षों तक मैं जो घिसटता रहा था, उस लकीर पीटने को 'काल-रेख' कहना ही मुझे रुच रहा था। परन्तु, कुछ काव्यात्मक स्फुरणा के वश, कुछ काल-अंतराल के प्रभाव-वश मैं अब इसे 'काल-क्रंदन' ही कहना अधिक समीचीन समझ रहा हूँ साहित्य -- और इसीलिए कविता भी -- जीवन के मूल की अर्थात् सत्य की खोज है: सत्य की परख, यथार्थ की परख! इसमें सब कुछ सुनने-सुनाने, गाने-गवाने ही योग्य है, ऐसा दावा मैं नहीं करता। परन्तु, क्या पढ़ने-पढ़ाने योग्य है, और क्या नहीं, इसका निर्णय भी तो मैं नहीं कर सकता; क्योंकि इसका कण-कण मेरा नितांत निजी सच है! इसमें कितना किस और किसी का भी सच प्रस्तुत है, यह निर्णय उन्हीं पर!

### *अननुभूत काल* (कविता-संग्रह)

अब यह तीसरी काव्य-पुस्तक है! एकदम नवीन काल से सम्बंधित! अभी-अभी हो गुज़रे बड़े

मानवीय हादसे को रेखांकित करती हुई: कोरोना की महा-आपदा! विश्व-आपदा! जो न कभी हुई थी, और आशा एवम् प्रार्थना ही कर सकते हैं, न कभी भविष्य में होगी! एकदम नये रूप में दुनिया को सोचने को मजबूर होना पड़ा: 'ऐसा भी हो सकता है?' बेतहाशा भागम-भाग में लगी दुनिया अचानक रुक-सी गयी; नहीं, रुक ही गयी — शब्दशः। वायुयान रुक गये, रेलयान रुक गये, बसें रुक गयीं, सारे वाहन रुक गये। मंदिर, मस्जिद, गुरुद्वारे और चर्च भी बंद हो गये: परमात्मा के घर थे वे! हैं! मक्का, मदीना बंद हो गये। वेटिकन बंद हो गया। वह चिरंतन अटूट आस्था जो रुकने का नाम नहीं लेती थी, और आए-दिन छोटी-छोटी बातों पर सिर-फुटव्वल को बेताब रहती थी, अचानक अपने को सकपकाता हुआ पाने लगी। क्या वह बस आस्था ही भर थी, दुनियावी प्राणियों को भरमाने के लिए; क्या उसमें कोई पारमार्थिक सार न था? तार्किक मन यह सोचने को विवश हो गया। इस कोरोना-काल ने बहुत सारे पाखण्ड-मण्डन किये हैं!

### *अम्बेडकर-स्मृति* (नाटिका)

जाति की समस्या भारत देश के लिए भयंकर होती जा रही है। यह जाति ही है जिसके चलते भारत-भूमि आक्रांताओं के समक्ष प्रणत हो गयी थी। कड़वी सच्चाई यह है कि राजनीतिक चतुराई के चलते 'सत्ताधीशों' ने अपने आप को 'ऊँचा' और सत्ता से 'वंचित' जनों को 'नीचा' मानना शुरू कर दिया। 'आज़ादी' के अधकचरे प्रयोग के चलते स्थिति और भी भयावह हो गयी है; 'नीचे लोग' ऊँचे लोगों को गरियाते रहते हैं: उसके लिए वे 'मनु-स्मृति' नाम की किसी पौराणिक पुस्तक को गरियाते रहते हैं, जबकि वास्तविकता यह है कि आधुनिक भारत के 99.99 प्रतिशत लोगों ने उस पुस्तक का पढ़ना तो दूर, नाम तक नहीं सुना है। उधर, नये सत्ताधीशों ने नयी स्मृति लिखकर -- संविधान लिखकर (जिसकी ड्राफ्टिंग समिति के अध्यक्ष होने के नाते अम्बेडकर को श्रेय मिला हुआ है) – पूर्ववर्ती समाज-व्यवस्था एवं अर्थ-व्यवस्था को एक सिरे से नकार और नेस्तनाबूद कर दिया है। समाज के बीच इस पर जो बहस चल रही है, उसी का एक छोटा सा नमूना है यह एकांकी!

### *प्रिय-प्रवास* (संकलन, 'हरिऔध' के महाकाव्य का)

'प्रिय-प्रवास' हिंदी -- खड़ी बोली -- का प्रथम महाकाव्य है, जो स्वनाम धन्य महाकवि अयोध्या सिंह उपाध्याय 'हरिऔध' की अमर कृति है। अत्यंत सुमधुर काव्य के रूप में युग-पुरुष श्रीकृष्ण के गोकुल से मथुरा प्रवास और उनके वियोग से व्यथित गोकुल-वासियों की विरह-वेदना का सरस चित्रण इसमें है। वह एक प्रकार से हर प्राणी की वेदना ही है, जो वह उस समय अनुभव करता है जब कोई स्वजन प्रवास हेतु जाता है या प्रयाण करता है, जो कि संसृति का अपरिहार्य लक्षण ही है। आसक्ति, मोह और ममता सब दुःखों का मूल है; जबकि ज्ञान दुःखों से मुक्ति का साधन! इस महा-आख्यान का यही सार अथच् केंद्रीय संदेश समझ में आता है! 'प्रिय-प्रवास' विरह, बिछुड़ने की वेदना, नैसर्गिक प्रेम और विश्व-कल्याण के संदेश का ही महाकाव्यात्मक सरस रूप है। 'विदेह' अरविन्द कुमार ने इस अद्भुत साहित्यिक कृति को पुनर्संकलित एवं पुनर्मुद्रित करके इसकी एक संक्षिप्त गद्य-कथा भी इसमें प्रस्तुत की है।

### *प्रार्थना एवं प्राणांश* (संकलित प्रेरक काव्यांश)

बहुत ही सरस और सार्थक प्रार्थनाओं एवं प्रेरणादायी काव्यांशों का संचयन है यह! जो न जाने कहाँ-कहाँ से 'विदेह' अरविंद कुमार ने अपनी रुचि अनुकूल संकलित एवं सम्पादित किया है, उन सभी मनीषियों के प्रति हार्दिक आभार व्यक्त करते हुए, जिनकी रचनाएँ और रचनाओं के प्राणांश इसमें संकलित किये गये हैं। जीवन, मृत्यु के वाहन के आगमन की प्रतीक्षा में रत यात्री के कार्य-कलाप और मनोदशा के अतिरिक्त और क्या है! इस प्रतीक्षा में क्या-क्या अनहोनी अनुभूतियाँ नहीं होतीं! इस प्रतीक्षा को कम कष्टकर करने के लिए काव्य-शास्त्र अनुश्रवण की अनुशंसा मनीषियों ने की है। साथ ही, प्रार्थना के माहात्म्य को भी स्वीकारा है।

*'मनो पुब्बंगमा धम्मा, मनो सेट्ठा मनोमया!'*
भगवान बुद्ध ने मन से ही सृजित होता हुआ इस सकल प्रपञ्च को बताया है। अत: मन को शुचि एवं निष्कंप रखकर आप संसार का अनुभव बदल सकते हैं। जब सभी कुछ कल्पित है, तो सबको अपना मत अनुभव जैसा ही लगता है। परन्तु, है

वस्तुतः सब कुछ कपोल-कल्पित ही: न इसे सत्य कहने का कोई तात्पर्य है, न असत्य कहने का! बस मन को साधने का साधनभर है प्रार्थना!

*महामुनि वाल्मीकि रचित् इतिहास : उत्तरकाण्ड (वाल्मीकि के उत्तरकाण्ड का गद्यांतरित सारांश)*

'रामायण' आदिकाव्य है, न केवल भारतवर्ष का, अपितु सकल मानव-समाज का भी। महर्षि वाल्मीकि-कृत यह काव्य-पुस्तक वस्तुतः तत्कालीन इतिहास है: उस राजवंश का, जिसकी कीर्ति हज़ारों वर्ष पश्चात् भी आज तक अक्षुण्ण है। उस राजवंश के तत्कालीन यशस्वी सम्राट 'राम' का इसमें वर्णन है। राम-राज्य की व्यवस्था, जिसका वर्णन ऋषि ने किया है, आज भी शासन-व्यवस्था के हेतु आदर्श मानी जाती है।

लेखक ने संस्कृत के ग्रंथ का मात्र सार रूप यहाँ प्रस्तुत किया है; सब प्रकार की काव्यात्मकता और अतिशयोक्तियों का निवारण करते हुए। साथ ही, आलंकारिकता को आधुनिक संदर्भों से जोड़ते हुए ऐतिहासिक-वैज्ञानिक अर्थों में भी विषय को समझाने का प्रयास किया है।

कितना यह किसको भाता है, यह तो हर व्यक्ति की अपनी-अपनी रुचि और सोच पर निर्भर करेगा; बहरहाल, लेखक ने अपना दृष्टिकोण प्रस्तुत किया है, वह भी इस चिन्ता से कि नयी पीढ़ी अपनी बहुमूल्य विरासत – गौरवशाली इतिहास -- की ओर एकदम ध्यान नहीं दे रही है। उसका एक कारण ग्रंथों का संस्कृत में होना, और दूसरा अत्यधिक प्रतीकात्मक होने के कारण कपोल-कल्पित-सा लगना, भी हो सकता है; उसी कारण का निवारण करने का यह विनीत प्रयास है।

*XXX*

## लेखक-परिचय

'विदेह' अरविन्द कुमार

भारतीय साहित्य की उदात्त पीठिका को आधुनिक संदर्भों से संपृक्त करने वाले सारस्वत साधक एवं विशिष्ट लेखन-शैली के प्रणेता वरिष्ठ साहित्यकार श्री अरविन्द कुमार 'विदेह' का जन्म 6 अप्रैल 1957 ई को उत्तर प्रदेश के गौतमबुद्धनगर जनपद की जेवर तहसील के छोटे-से गाँव 'मारहरा' में हुआ था। आपके माता-पिता की मानव-मूल्यों में गहरी आस्था रही है। सीमित संसाधनों, बल्कि विपन्नता, के बावजूद भी आप सफलता के लाभी हुए। आपने तत्कालीन आगरा विश्वविद्यालय के अलीगढ़ स्थित धर्मसमाज कॉलेज से भौतिक विज्ञान में स्नातकोत्तर उपाधि प्राप्त की है। आप देश के प्रतिष्ठित बैंक – भारतीय स्टेट बैंक – में दीर्घकालीन सेवा प्रदान करने के

उपरांत दिसम्बर, 2018 में सहायक महाप्रबंधक के पद से सेवा निवृत्त हुए हैं।

श्री 'विदेह' छात्र-जीवन से ही अत्यंत मेधावी रहे हैं। विज्ञान-संवर्ग के विद्यार्थी होते हुए भी आपकी साहित्य के प्रति गहरी अभिरुचि रही है। साहित्य के प्रति आपका अनुराग इतना प्रबल रहा है कि बैंकिंग सेक्टर में अति व्यस्त जीवन-शैली वाली नौकरी करते हुए भी आप साहित्य और लेखन से अनवरत रूप से जुड़े रहे हैं। उनकी रचनाएँ तत्कालीन 'कादम्बिनी' जैसी लब्ध-प्रतिष्ठ पत्रिकाओं में काफ़ी पहले छप चुकी हैं; और उनके अन्य लेख एवं कविताएँ अन्य हिंदी, अंग्रेज़ी पत्र-पत्रिकाओं में यदा-कदा छपते रहे हैं। साथ ही, आपने हिंदी एवं अंग्रेजी भाषा के साहित्य का विशद अध्ययन एवं सृजन किया है। संस्कृत एवं पाली भाषा के साहित्य में भी आपकी गहरी अभिरुचि है।

विभिन्न विधाओं में आपने अब तक 27 ग्रंथों का प्रणयन किया है, जिनमें 17 अंग्रेजी एवं 10 हिंदी भाषा में हैं। हिंदी की पुस्तकों में 03 कहानी-संग्रह (अनपढ़ लिपि, पाषाण युग, निसर्ग); 03 कविता-संग्रह (आर्त-गान, काल-क्रन्दन, अननुभूत काल); 01 नाटिका (अम्बेडकर-स्मृति); 01 काव्य-संचयन (प्रार्थना एवं प्राणांश)

उल्लेखनीय हैं। इसके अतिरिक्त आपने खड़ी बोली के प्रथम महाकाव्य 'प्रिय-प्रवास' को भी पुनर्संकलित एवं पुनर्मुद्रित किया है; तथा साथ ही, वाल्मीकि रामायण के उत्तरकाण्ड का गद्यांतरण इतिहास के दृष्टिकोण से आपने 'महामुनि वाल्मीकि रचित् इतिहास: रामायण – उत्तरकाण्ड' नामक पुस्तक के रूप में किया है।

अंग्रेजी भाषा में आपकी उपन्यास श्रृंखला 'Hypocrisy & Reality' है जिसके अब तक 9 खण्ड वह प्रस्तुत कर चुके हैं (Beyond the Pale; Wilderness of Literacy; Advent of Time; Devoid of Shelter; Price of Refuge; Hatred towards Love; Towards the *Yoga*; On the Descent; In the Exile)। इसके अतिरिक्त, 01 Comedietta (*Chambellion*); 01 Short Story collection (Brainy Beasts); 01 Poetry anthology (Bewailing Muse); 01 Drama (Self-styled Sovereign, the Judiciary); पौराणिक ग्रंथ 'शिव-पुराण' के आधुनिक संदर्भों में अध्ययन पर आधारित 01 पुस्तक (Procreation, the Adorable); 2017 के साहित्य नोबेल पुरस्कार विजेता, Kazuo Ishiguro, के प्रथम उपन्यास 'A Pale View of the Hills' पर आधारित 01 समीक्षात्मक ग्रंथ (Nagasaki: Bomb & Aftermath) हैं।

'विदेह' जितने मौलिक सर्जक हैं उतने ही समर्थ अनुवादक भी हैं। उन्होंने हिंदी के 02 काव्य-संग्रहों – 'निर्विकार' मुकेश के 'हत्यारी सदी में जीवन की खोज', और 'अश्वघोष' ओमप्रकाश शर्मा के 'अदृश्य का यथार्थ' – का काव्यात्मक अनुवाद अंग्रेजी में किया है, जो क्रमश: 'Search for Life' एवं 'Reality of Invisible' के नाम से प्रकाशित हुई हैं।

'विदेह' के व्यक्तित्व का निर्माण घोर विपन्नता और कठोर संघर्षों ने किया है, जिसका प्रभाव उनकी लेखन-शैली पर निर्भीक अभिव्यक्ति और बेवाकी के रूप में देखा जा सकता है। आपके जीवन का अनुभव अत्यन्त व्यापक रहा है। आपने विपन्नता भी भोगी है, और सुख-सुविधा-सम्पन्न अमेरिकी जीवन भी जीया है; साथ ही, अनेक विदेश-यात्राओं का भी आपको अनुभव है।

केवल साहित्य ही नहीं, 'विदेह' की प्रवृत्तियों में ध्यान-साधना, विपश्यना, योग-साधना, प्राकृतिक-जीवन, आरोग्य, शाकाहार, बागवानी, पर्यटन और पैदल भ्रमण भी सम्मिलित हैं।

2024 के हिंदी दिवस पर – 14 सितंबर को – 'विदेह' को 'शुभम् साहित्य, कला एवम् संस्कृति संस्थान' द्वारा उनके सर्वोच्च सम्मान 'शुभम् रत्न' से सम्मानित किया गया।

'विदेह' की पुस्तकें 'Notion Press', Blue Rose One, Amazon और Flipkart पर तीनों ही प्रारूपों – ebooks, paperback एवम् hard cover – में उपलब्ध हैं।

XXX

## About the Author

*'Videh' Arvind Kumar*

An unflinching adorer of the goddess of wisdom, the *Saraswatee*, and the one who has associated the lofty traditions of Indian literature with the present day contexts, and also, an author of an uncanny style of his own, the seasoned litterateur, *'Videh' Arvind Kumar,* was born on 6th of April, 1957, at a hamlet called *'Maar-Haraa'* in *Jewar Tehseel* of *Gautam Buddha Nagar* distt. in UP. His parents were staunch votaries of human values. Despite unbearable financial constraints, rather extreme wretchedness, he overcame the hurdles of existence and succeeded. He is a post-graduate in Physics from D S College, *Aleegarh,* affiliated to the then *Aagaraa* University. He retired as an Asstt General Manager from the esteemed Bank – State Bank of India – after putting in a long as well as illustrious service there.

*'Videh'* has been meritorious ever since his school days. Despite being a science stream scholar, he has been showing a keen interest in literature all along. His bonding with literature has been so strong that notwithstanding his pursuing such a busy job as Banking, he managed to sustain his love for literature. His works have been published decades back in the then esteemed magazines such as *'Kaadambinee'*. Also, his stray articles and compositions have found place in various magazines and journals now and then. Besides, he has been a voracious reader of literature and other stuff both in *Hindee* and English languages, apart from himself being a prolific writer and a poet. He is also an adorer of the literature in *Sanskrit* and *Pali* languages.

In variegated genre he has composed as many as 27 books so far, of which, 17 are in English and 10 in *Hindee*. Among the *Hindee* books, there are 03 story anthologies (*Anapadh Lipi; Paashaan Yug; Nisarg*); 03 poetry anthologies (*Aaart Gaan; Kaal Krandan; Ananubhoot Kaal*); 01 drama (*Ambedkar Smriti*); 01 collection of select poetic pieces (*Praarthanaa evam Praanaansh)*. Aside of this, he has compiled, commented, edited and got re-published the first epic of the *Khadee Bolee Hindee*, the *Priya Pravaas*; and a book entitled *'Mahaamuni Vaalmeeki Rachit Itihaas: Raamaayan -- Uttar Kaand'* which presents, in succinct prose form, the ancient history of India as narrated in the most ancient epic.

As regards English oeuvre of *'Videh'*, he has so far published 9 volumes of the long fiction series 'Hypocrisy & Reality' (Beyond the Pale; Wilderness of Literacy; Advent of Time; Devoid of Shelter; Price of Refuge; Hatred towards Love; Towards the *Yoga*; On the Descent; In the Exile) with yet more planned to come. Besides, 01 Comedietta (*Chambellion*); 01 Short Story collection (Brainy Beasts); 01 Poetry anthology (Bewailing Muse); 01 Drama (Self-Styled Sovereign, the Judiciary); 01 book based on the study of mythological volume *'Shiva Puraan'* in the present day context (Procreation, the Adorable); 01 commentary book on the first novel – 'A Pale View of the Hills' -- of the 2017 Nobel Literature laureate, Kazuo Ishiguro (Nagasaki: Bomb & Aftermath) are other books.

Not only an original writer as well as thinker, but also, a capable and versatile translator is *'Videh'* inasmuch as he has translated in English free verse form 02 *Hindee* poetry anthologies, viz. *'Hatyaaree Sadee Mein Jeevan Kee Khoj'* of *'Nirvikaar'* Mukesh Kumaar, and *'Adrishya Kaa Yathaarth'* of *'Ashwaghosh'* Omprakaash Sharmaa with the titles of the books being *seriatim* as 'Search for Life' and 'Reality of Invisible'.

The persona of *'Videh'* has been moulded by constant struggles and abject adversities, which have metamorphosed into his style of narration being quite frank as well as bland, if only straightforward.

His experiences of life are multifarious. He has not only suffered the pangs of extreme poverty and adversity in his childhood, but also, enjoyed the comforts and pleasures of the modern world by living in America. Besides, he has visited and toured in various foreign countries, too.

Not only in literature, but also, in exotic pursuits like meditation, spiritual practice, *Vipashyanaa, Yoga* practice, naturopathy, natural living, *Aarogya,* vegetarianism, gardening, tourism and long walks on foot *'Videh'* is equally active.

To add to his laurels, *'Videh'* has been honoured with their highest honour *'Shubham Ratna'* by the institution *'Shubham Saahitya, Kalaa Evam Sanskriti Sansthaan'* on the occasion of *Hindee Divas*, i.e. on 14th September, 2024.

The books of *'Videh'* are available in all the three formats, viz. eBooks, paperbacks and hardcovers from the Notion Press, Blue Rose One, Amazon and the Flipkart.

XXX